# BLIT

*and other sto*

# BLITZ
## and other stories

## Esther Kreitman

*Translated from
Yiddish by Dorothee van Tendeloo*

*Edited by Sylvia Paskin*

DAVID
PAUL

Published in 2004
by David Paul
29 Redston Road, London N8 7HL
www.davidpaulbooks.com

First published by the Narod Press in London in 1950
in Yiddish as *Yikhes: Dertseylungen un Skitsen*

Translated from the Yiddish by Dorothee van Tendeloo

Worldwide distribution (except North America) by Central Books, 99 Wallis Road,
London E9 5LN

A CIP catalogue of this book is available from the British Library

ISBN 0-9540542-5-3

*My Uncle Yitzhak*, reprinted from *Commentary*,
December 1992, by permission; all rights reserved

Front cover: painting by Abram Games, 1937, copyright © the Estate of Abram Games

Printed in Great Britain by Biddles Ltd, King's Lynn

*Esther Kreitman*

# Acknowledgements

A heartfelt, sadly, posthumous thanks to Esther Kreitman's son Maurice Carr whom we met in Paris aged 89, in December 2002, shortly before his death. He not only gave us his permission to publish *Blitz and other stories* but the blessing of his goodwill, kindness and knowledge of Yiddish literature. He felt, as we did, that translating his mother's work was an important task and he was thrilled that *Yikhes* was going to appear in English. He also showed us that there is much fine Yiddish literature that merits translation. Our thanks too to Lola Carr for her hospitality, and to Hazel Carr for her support, for sharing with us her father's unpublished memoir and for allowing us to republish "My Uncle Yitzhak". We are indebted to our translator, Dorothee van Tendeloo, for bringing this book to our attention, and for her efforts to produce a thoughtful translation, that Maurice Carr himself felt would be faithful to the original. A special thank you to Dafna Clifford for her advice for this project, for sharing her knowledge of Esther Kreitman with us, for making us aware of the vastness of Yiddish and for helping us appreciate the *hutzpa* of our undertaking, and we are grateful for the draft of her article on Esther Kreitman that appeared in *Prooftexts* magazine. We are also grateful to Naomi Games for the use of her father's painting on the front cover.

DP and SP

*This book is dedicated to the memory of
Maurice Carr
(1913-2003)*

# A Note on the Translation

In general, Yiddish words have been transliterated using the standard spelling recommended by the YIVO Institute for Jewish Research. We haven't done this in cases where it might cause confusion, or where words have officially recognised English spellings. So for example we say *Yom Kippur* not *Yom Kiper*. And we use *challah* instead of *khale* for a braided loaf, as it would appear more familiar to English-speaking readers. Yet the sound of "kh" in Yiddish and that of the "ch" in words from Hebrew are similar: guttural, clearing of the throat sounds that have no equivalent in English.

Yiddish is an eclectic language that has developed over the last one thousand years. It is written in Hebrew script but borrows from Romance and Slavic languages and includes a large amount of German. Many sounds do differ from modern Hebrew. For instance, the "e" ending in words such as *bime* is like the sound in the English word "get", thus *bime* has two syllables and does not emphasise the preceding vowel. There are no silent letters.

Where Esther Kreitman used English words and phrases in the original Yiddish version of *Yikhes* we have italicised those words for added emphasis to indicate her occasional use of English.

# *Contents*

Introduction - Fifty Years On     xi

## The Shtetl Stories

The New World     3

A Silk Gabardine     11

Reb Meyerl     31

Shloyme     43

Jewish Nobility     51

## The London Stories

Jim     75

Breaking the Fast     83

Becoming a Tramp     89

Too Late     95

Two Libraries     107

She is Not Blind     111

Clocks     125

Blitz     131

Dogs     137

**Afterword:** My Uncle Yitzhak by Maurice Carr     143

Glossary     163

## Introduction

# Fifty Years On

Esther Kreitman (1891-1954) never achieved the same accolades for her fiction as her more famous younger brothers Isaac Bashevis Singer, who won the Nobel Prize for literature in 1978, and Israel Joshua Singer, did for theirs. Their reputations as great Yiddish writers have long overshadowed hers. Her brothers were more consistent in their achievements and prolific in their output.

Despite his sister's relatively small output, Isaac Bashevis, who was not always her greatest admirer, said: "I do not know of a single woman in Yiddish literature who wrote better than she did." He also acknowledged that it was through his sister that the first sparks of literary talent in the family were lit.

She wrote only two novels, *Der sheydim-tants* (The Demons' Dance) in 1936 - later translated into English in 1946 as *Deborah*, by her son Maurice Carr - and *Brilyantyn* (Diamonds) in 1944. Her only other known work are the short stories in this collection, originally published in 1950 in London in Yiddish as *Yikhes* (Jewish Nobility) and translated for the first time into English in this book.

Hinde Esther Singer was born in Bilgoraj, a *shtetl*, a small town, where many of the inhabitants were Jewish, near Lublin, Poland. She continued to write in Yiddish, the language spoken by Ashkenazi Jews of eastern European origin, long after she left Poland at the outbreak of the First World War. It was a journey which took her to Berlin, Antwerp and then on to London. Two decades later, her brothers departed for America. Perhaps she left Poland too early, before the emergence of a lively Yiddish women writers' scene in Warsaw where her work would have reached a wider and more appreciative audience. And, as we shall see, she had a difficult life, plagued by physical and mental ill health and an awkward personality which did not always endear her to those whom she met.

Her fame, till now, if it can be called such, rests on her being the model for Isaac Bashevis' story "Yentl, the Yeshiva Boy" - where a young woman disguises her gender and dresses as a man in order to get herself an education. The story became the basis for Barbra Streisand's film *Yentl* (1983) and mirrors the efforts of the young Hinde Esther to gain an independent education, which had been denied by her father, a rabbi, who frowned on secular learning.

On the fiftieth anniversary of her death it seems more than appropriate to reassess her status as a writer. Nearly forty years of her adult life were spent in London, from the outbreak of the First World War until her death. In calling this collection *Blitz*, we have set out to show that her work should be recognised as that of a British Yiddish writer albeit one who felt that her true self belonged in *die alte heim*, the old country.

According to Maurice Carr, his mother felt that "English-speaking Britain with its fogs, its monarchy, its lords, its dustmen, its pubs et al was something of a bad dream." Yet her descriptions of the bombing of the capital in the title story "Blitz" mark her out as a true Londoner. A more searing, powerful description of the terror and devastation of an air raid would be hard to find.

Most of the stories are set in London. Her adaptation to living in Britain is not only implicit in the characters and themes of the London-based stories but also in the very use of the language itself. We have italicised English words in the text, where they were originally written in English, to show how Hinde Esther's thoughts and speech were influenced by her adopted language even though she was writing in Yiddish. She uses English words, phrases and customs to especially good effect in the story "Too Late". She even translated books from English into Yiddish.

Hinde Esther was an acute observer of the impact of a changing world on the Jews who had come to live in Britain. And the way she describes her Jewish characters in London will resonate with present-day audiences. She demonstrates the tensions in the transition from one culture to another, and the delicious ironies in moving from tradition to modernity. For instance, the Jewish landlady in "Breaking the Fast" has bacon for breakfast, except on the fast day of Yom Kippur when she treats herself to chicken, but she despises her Jewish neighbour, old Borenstein, for blowing the shofar, a ram's horn, and disturbing her. The tenant she prefers, Mr Davies, with whom she spends her time gossiping, has a Christian mother and Jewish father and he joins the Salvation Army - to atone for the sin of his Jewish ancestry!

In "Too Late", she gleefully describes how the Segal's young guest from the old country surprises and embarrasses his hosts by speaking better English than they do. Mr Segal, a long-term resident in England, does not know Hebrew well enough to conduct the Friday night prayers properly and muddles up all the words. As if this were not enough, the newcomer needs lodging while he is training to be a specialist in Harley Street. But his host, Mr Segal, though wealthy, is just a common tailor.

The stories in the collection give ample evidence of Hinde Esther's considerable gifts as a storyteller. They show she had a fine gift of observation and a natural ear for dialogue - her characters pulsate with life whether they are in the process of being destroyed by a tragic destiny or experiencing brief moments of joy - the major motifs that run through the work. The original title *Yikhes* (Jewish Nobility) conveys Esther Kreitman's concern with family background and the burden of maintaining tradition, a theme she returns to again and again.

Her writing is fiercely autobiographical. She herself wryly intimated that the circumstances of her birth set the tone for her entire life. In "The New World", one of the most poignant of the stories, a baby still in her mother's womb tells of her own birth. In this extraordinary narrative, she imagines that her arrival will be met by rapture. Instead, she is rejected by her mother and grandmother, and ignored by her father because of her gender. Finally she is given to a wet nurse who takes her to her hovel of a home which the baby then shares with the woman's six children and husband. There is no room for the baby except under the table amongst the filth and cobwebs.

We know from Esther Kreitman's son, Maurice Carr (see his piece "My Uncle Yitzhak" at the end of this book), that this was the fate his mother endured. She was fostered for the first three years of her life and she blamed the atrocious conditions in which she was brought up, for the poor eyesight she suffered all her life.

The theme of seeing and not seeing is explored in various ways in her stories. Light or the lack of it is repeatedly mentioned. Hinde Esther's sense of rejection and the handicap of poor sight are inextricably linked.

In the powerful story, "She is Not Blind", a wife is abused and disregarded by her family because of her blundering near-sightedness. She appears to be weak and ailing, but nevertheless wields a strange power over her husband. Many characters in the stories are described as having weak, watery or bloodshot eyes or the visual qualities of their eyes are described with great intensity.

At the same time Hinde Esther can sketch a vivid scene with a few choice words and phrases. There are loving descriptions of the colour and beauty of flowers and gardens. It is noticeable too, in her use of adjectives which describe the myriad shades of flames and fire, that this no doubt gave her personal pleasure in life. She is almost compelled to describe the glisten and gleam of surfaces with reverence.

"Seeing" is also explored as a metaphor. So Bella, in "Clocks", only learns to see the danger she is in after a traumatic night in a shelter and "seeing" the office clock as if for the first time in a new and threatening light. In "Reb Meyerl", the rabbi cannot "see" what action to take to determine his future and lets Providence decide for him.

Poor sight was not the only legacy of Hinde Esther's early experiences. She also was born with a form of epilepsy. She regularly suffered fits and had bouts of depression. Her family did not understand her condition and she was considered over-emotional, unpredictable and hysterical. Maurice Carr, in an unpublished memoir, has written how his mother would foam at the mouth, collapse and writhe on the ground and then come to completely unaware of what had occurred. "She had frequent nightmares - *vilde haloimis*, wild dreams." Her brothers thought she was crazy. "Your mother was a madwoman," Bashevis told Maurice, who never forgave him for the remark. And Israel Joshua, whom she envied and admired, wrote, in 1943, in *Di Mishpokhe Kornovski* (The Family Carnovsky), of a pathetic spinster who is hopelessly out of touch with reality and compensates for her loneliness by identifying with the heroes of the romantic novels she reads all day.

Hinde Esther's deep sense of rejection by her family was also to dominate her life and was further compounded at an early age by the different way her brothers were treated. They were encouraged to study while she was not.

Ironically Bathsheve Singer, Hinde Esther's mother, had been allowed to develop her intellectual gifts, by her own father, Reb Mordechai, the rabbi of Bilgoraj who had enjoyed engaging with her in discussions of Jewish exegesis. Reb Mordechai was a *misnaged*, an adversary of the mystical Hasidic movement. But, disastrously, he had paired Hinde Esther's mother with the feckless Pinkhos Menahem, who had the *yikhes*, the equivalent of Jewish nobility, by being a descendent of Yosef Caro, the medieval codifier of Jewish law, who could trace his lineage back to King David. Pinkhos Menahem was a Talmudic scholar and kabbalist, he loved the ecstatic dancing of the Hasidim but lacked the intellectual rigour of Reb Mordechai. He struggled to make a living as a rabbi. According to Maurice Carr, his grandfather was: "weak and submissive, which is what a *wife* should be." The marriage was a complete mismatch.

Reb Pinkhos Menahem blamed his wife's free spirit and disinterest in the home on her education and was determined not to make the same mistake with his daughter, Hinde Esther. But she refused to accept the role of domestic drudge. In the autobiographical novel *Deborah*, Esther Kreitman's heroine fights against her family's treatment of her as the author herself had done: "Ever since childhood she had longed to receive an education, to cease being the nonentity of the family. She would learn things, gain understanding and then not only would Papa be a great Talmudist, not only would her mother possess a boundless store of knowledge, not only would Michael be a brilliant student, but she, Deborah - the girl who as her father had once said was to be a mere nobody when she grew up - would be a person of real consequence."

Hinde Esther eventually taught herself and defiantly went to evening classes and joined study groups and debating and socialist societies in Warsaw. Isaac Bashevis described her as a "Hasid in skirts" for her love of learning and her rebelliousness. No doubt, this thought occurred to him when devising the "Yentl" character. Perhaps he was also projecting his own ambiguity towards Hasidism, which Hinde Esther did not espouse but which flows through her work almost seamlessly, often unexpectedly - as in the association of the sound of an air raid warning siren with a song of lamentation in the story "*Blitz*", or in describing the excitement in the marketplace on the eve of Passover in "Shloyme". These descriptions reveal a tenderness towards the customs and traditions that so nearly obscured her talent.

Many of Hinde Esther's female characters in *"Blitz"* are forced to make their own decisions and throughout her stories they seek an independent life to escape stultifying personal circumstances or traditional customs whether they be in London or the *shtetl*s of Poland.

This was a reflection of what she herself did - remove herself from her environment by agreeing to an arranged marriage with a man whom she had not met and whom she never loved. On being told by her mother Bathsheve that her parents had found a match for her in Avrom Kreitman, she replied: "You wish to see the back of me. Very well, I shall go into exile." This was a reckless act of self-destructiveness that was to haunt her for the rest of her days but was to become a fruitful source for her fiction.

In "The Silk Gabardine" Royze's distress at having to marry against her will when she is in love with a Gentile makes her mad with grief on her wedding day, forcing her father to abandon the match. And in "Jewish Nobility", Toybe runs off to make her own marriage with an "unsuitable" suitor on the very day of her sister's wedding to an acceptable match.

After marrying in Berlin the Kreitmans went to live in Antwerp, where Avrom Kreitman worked as a diamond cutter. They left for London to escape the horrors of the First World War and Hinde Esther effectively remained there for the rest of her life with occasional forays to Antwerp and Poland. When in England Avrom returned to the Russian land he had left earlier to avoid army service and was conscripted into the tsar's army. Later he was employed by the Bolsheviks "to serve notice on the rich to clear out their homes," as he told Hinde Esther and young Maurice on his return.

Long absences from each other were then to characterise the rest of the marriage. Hinde Esther often left her husband in a search for intellectual stimulation and recognition and sometimes because of nervous breakdowns, yet she always returned to him and used his name almost like a *nom de plume* for her literary work. At least she was no longer a Singer and had a name of her own for her writing.

But they were poor. Avrom Kreitman was mostly out of work as a diamond cutter. He eventually did find work as a maker of frames for ladies' handbags. But he could not be relied on to be the provider. On one occasion, Hinde Esther was forced to pawn her fur stole and a diamond brooch and also had to sell her pearls. She even had a short-lived career as a shopkeeper running a small grocery store.

In his unpublished memoir Maurice Carr details their living conditions in various attic homes in north London - in Henry Road, Petherton Road, Clephane Road, Beresford Road and Lordship Park, often amongst other refugee families of various degrees of eccentricity. He describes his mother trying to earn money by "stringing coloured beads into necklaces and bracelets." She is also forced to embroider "on silk blouses the flowers which pay the rent and our keep, wearing a pince-nez." Eventually "the poor light even with the curtains thrust aside is a strain on her eyes. She cannot carry on much longer as the family breadwinner."

It comes as no surprise that one of Hinde Esther's major pre-occupations as a writer is an examination of poverty and its travails. The London stories are full of this seemingly hopeless struggle against want. Jim, the hero, in the story of that name, is a human horse working to deliver his cartload of boxes to the factory in the rain-soaked city. He feels jealous at the sight of a gleaming Daimler with a leather-gloved chauffeur. Bill, in "Becoming a Tramp", has been wounded fighting in the war and has tuberculosis. He is forced to go from one job to another to support his somewhat wayward wife and four lively sons. In "Dogs", Tom Dickson and his wife do not have enough money for rent or food, or clothes for their small, sickly baby but bet their last shillings at the greyhound track. The chicken slaughterer, Reb Borenstein, in "Breaking the Fast", lives in a couple of shabby rooms despised by his landlady. Outside in the Lane the women bicker and fight in search of bargains. The Jews, in "Two Libraries", huddle for warmth and company as they doze in the Jewish library. The aspiring Yiddish writer in "She is Not Blind" must hawk his own books with little or no success.

By contrast to these conditions, Esther Kreitman is scathing about the Jews who have left the East End for the salubrious suburbs, mocking the upwardly mobile Segals in "Too Late" who for all their luxurious furniture and sumptuous lifestyle cannot buy a husband for their eldest daughter with the very "English" name of Shirley. There are three kinds of race-goer in "Dogs" - the poor who spend their last pennies, the rich, who arrive in cars with "stiff hats on their greased heads and white gloves on their kosher hands" and "young Jewish men who only yesterday were reading prayer books and who today are petit bourgeois". Bella, in "Clocks", is a well-turned-out young lady with polished red nails and glossy hair and an elegant handbag who works in an office. She looks after her appearance and no doubt her future. Madame Zesha, in "She is Not Blind", voluptuous and golden-haired, bears the fruit of three marriages and three widowhoods in her capacious handbag. Adorned with jewellery and a magnificent décolleté, she urges her niece Perele to make a bid for a new life in America, to escape bombed-out London and find a rich husband.

The inhabitants of the *shtetl* are also ground down by poverty, whether of the spirit or materially. Yidel yearns to wear the correct garb in "A Silk Gabardine" so he can sit alongside the wealthier members of his congregation with equanimity, but his dream ends in misery for his family. In "Jewish Nobility", Hershel's frantic desire to marry one daughter off to a wealthy husband causes him to neglect the other, for which he pays a heavy price. Young Shloyme in the story of that name, begs on the street like a dog to feed himself even though he shames his family in the process.

Hinde Esther's experience of poverty, her left-wing leanings, and her increasing ease with English led her to translate two English classics into Yiddish, Charles Dickens' *A Christmas Carol* and George Bernard Shaw's *The Intelligent Woman's Guide to Socialism*.

The relationship between Jews and non-Jews is a theme explored by Hinde Esther in the *shtetl* stories and questions of Jewish identity arise in the London tales. In "A Silk Gabardine", Yidel has to move house because he finds his daughter Royze locked in an embrace with a Gentile lad, and in "Jewish Nobility" one of the characters, Mendel, marries out of the Jewish religion, changes his name to Matchek and is ill-treated by his Polish wife who calls him "a filthy Jew". He becomes a stranger to his family and is only mourned by his mother. In the story "Jim", the hero only remembers his Jewish heritage on his weddingday, with confusing results: "When he was about to put his signature on the wedding documents, his skinny hand suddenly trembled: he remembered he was a Jew... He kept hearing a voice in his head, saying 'Jew', 'Goy', 'Jew', 'Goy' - he did not know himself what he wanted."

Esther Kreitman was possessed by these two separate worlds - the one she escaped from and the one she propelled herself towards: Jewish

London, her "new world", and the *alte heim,* the "old world" of the *shtetls* of Poland where she grew up. The stories in *Blitz* are divided almost evenly between these two places but neither place offers respite or happiness; they are both fraught with problems of survival - material and spiritual. In life too Hinde Esther never truly found a "home".

We can see this clearly in Maurice Carr's memoir. He describes the customers' attitude to his beloved "mama Hindele": "They patronise my mother for her *alte heim* anecdotes. If only she wouldn't tinge her reminiscences with the *yikhes* of the Singer family, all would be well. Oh, how I wish my short-sighted mother could see as I see that sour-sweet blend of amused scepticism and heartfelt compassion on her customers' faces! These ladies wheedle me for information about my father, on whom they have never set eyes. I shrug off as if beyond my comprehension their fishwife Yiddish, I look askance at their halting English and I shrink from the tip they try to thrust into the hand of the fairy-tale-spinning grocery-woman's nitwit son."

It is possible that living in London and Antwerp did not help Hinde Esther gain recognition for her work. The London Yiddish literary scene was a small circle. The struggle for acceptance must have had a depressing effect on her self-confidence. Yet she was a dedicated participant in the Whitechapel writers' circle that kept the flame alive, of Yiddish language and literature, among the refugees. Hinde Esther was a friend of Stencl, the leading London-based Yiddish poet, and was in correspondence with Yiddish writers all over the world.

She was encouraged by Stefan Zweig, who wrote to her in 1939 not to lose heart in the face of the prevailing indifference among English publishers to books set in a Jewish milieu. The Yiddish writer in "She is Not Blind" who hawks his own books around, without success, was clearly based on herself and her literary friends. She sold her novels from her home in Lordship Park and struggled with the practical difficulties of selling them abroad, as neither she nor the booksellers could afford the postage.

Esther Kreitman did not achieve happiness or contentment in her life. She was married to a *shlemiel,* an awkward misfit - Maurice Carr's description. She was often ill and depressed, slighted by her family she had to transcend the barriers of gender, and background.

It is clear she saw slights where none were intended, which kept people at a distance from her. A young Chimen Abramsky, who later became an expert on Judaica, remembers meeting Esther Kreitman. She told him he didn't like her even though he had given her no evidence for this. At the time she had been living with his mother-in-law, a bookseller, at her home in Highgate, in London, where she gave refuge to people in distress. It was one of several occasions that Hinde Esther had run away from her husband.

Her suffering was made worse because the literary world was more enamoured of her brothers' works. Nevertheless her achievement was not inconsiderable. Apart from *Blitz*, her novel *Deborah* is a remarkable autobiographical account of the lives of the Singer family and the travails of the young Hinde Esther, a.k.a. Deborah, and her struggle to be free. Her other work, the only one yet to be translated into English, *Brilyantyn* (Diamonds), explores the unravelling of a Jewish family against the backdrop of a modern city and the diamond cutters of Antwerp and Hatton Garden. It is our intention to bring out *Brilyantyn*, in translation, in the near future and then, perhaps, the work of Esther Kreitman will have been completed and she will have achieved the recognition for her work that she so richly deserves.

David Paul and Sylvia Paskin
London, 2004

# The Shtetl Stories

# The New World

I first felt unhappy while lying in my mother's belly. It was so hot! I twisted around, curled up and pretended not to be there. That's how it was for me.

Then, five months later, when I started to feel stirrings of life, it really got to me. I was bored stiff by the whole affair! I was truly fed up. Most of all, I was tired of lying in the dark all the time and I protested. But who could hear me? Crying was no good. So one day, after coming to the conclusion that my tears were useless, I began to look for other ways to free myself.

I wanted only one thing - to get out.

After some considerable thought, I realised that the best thing for me to do was to start fighting with my mother. So I began throwing myself around, stamping with rage, often poking her in the ribs: nothing could stop me, but it was all to no avail. The only result was that I got myself a bad name so that, for instance, whenever I got tired of lying on one side, and would turn over, to be a little more comfortable, they would start grumbling. Well, to cut a long story short, I did not get anywhere. I had to lie there the whole nine months - all the way to the end!

So, I comforted myself, as I did not have any choice, I would have to get used to coming out later. When, eventually, they let me out into God's world, I would already know how to behave.

I had no doubts that I would be an important guest. There were several reasons. First of all, I would often hear my mother talking to some woman or other, who later turned out to be my grandmother.

"It hurts a little, but I hardly feel it," my mother said repeatedly. "I am so happy. Oh, I used to be so afraid of being barren. Do you believe me? Two years after the wedding, and there was still nothing to show for it. Minke, the barren, was also convinced that she would give birth one day. So I thought, why should I be any luckier than her?"

"Well, praise be! With God's help it will all come to pass in good time; and the evil eye, God forbid, will not interfere," was the standard answer of my grandmother.

From such conversations, I gathered that I would be a welcome guest.

I knew that here in the other world, where I lived as a soul, whenever an important person was about to enter, everybody prepared to receive him with pomp and ceremony. First of all, an enormous brightness would spread itself throughout the heavens. Angels would be flying in to welcome him: merry, resplendent, and cloaked in bright sunlight. He would be surrounded by celebrating cherubs who radiated such holy joy that the person could only regret he had not died earlier. It is therefore no surprise that I, an important, long-awaited guest, expected to be born in a big, bright house where the sunlight would be streaming through the open windows.

I was looking forward to being greeted every morning by a multitude of birds singing me their song. Moreover, I was to be born on the first of *Adar* - a month of joy in the Hebrew calendar. "When *Adar* begins, people rejoice."

But here it comes - my first disappointment.

My mother is lying in a tiny room, an alcove. The bedroom is draped with dark curtains, which keep out even the smallest ray of light. The little window has been tightly shut, so that, God forbid, no fresh air can creep in. One must not catch a cold. The birds are, apparently, not very keen on barred light and closed windows, so they have gone elsewhere to look for a better, freer place in which to sing. In the meantime, there is not much happiness to speak of, since I have turned out to be a girl, and everybody in the room is disappointed, even my mother.

In short, there is no happiness at all. I am already almost half an hour old, but apart from a few slaps from some woman as I came into the world, no one looks at me. I feel so alone!

My grandmother comes in and smiles at my mother. She seems overjoyed - probably because her daughter has come through her ordeal all right. There is not so much as a glance in my direction.

"*Mazl tov* to you, my daughter, that you may live!"

"*Mazl tov*, that one may live with good fortune!"

My mother smiles too, but not at me.

"I would have been happier if it had been a boy," says my mother. My grandmother winks roguishly and comforts her: "It doesn't matter, there will be boys too."

I find it hard to believe all the things that are being said. What was I born for, if all this joy had nothing to do with me! I am already sick of it all. Oh, how I want to go back to the other world!

Suddenly I feel a strange chill all over my body and my thoughts are swept aside. I feel myself clasped between two big, fleshy hands, which lift me up in the air. I am shaking all over. Maybe - a frightening thought occurs to me - maybe they are going to put me back in for another few months? Brrr! The very idea makes me shiver.

But then something makes my head swim and everything is spinning round me. I am completely soaked, tiny as I am! Am I in a river? But no, a river is cool and pleasant, whereas I feel slightly scalded. But that doesn't bother me as much as my fear of what those two big, clumsy hands are going to do with me. I am completely in their power.

Thank God! I have been taken out of the water. They carry me back into the alcove, all dried and dressed. Then I am passed around the room, everybody takes a look at me, says a few words. Finally, I am put back to bed. My mother puts some kind of sweet, liquid thing in my mouth; I am really hungry for what the world has to offer.

My mother looks at me with kind, soft eyes, and it warms my heart. A sweet fatigue comes over me and soon I am lost in a happy dream...but my happiness doesn't last long. I have been brutally woken up by somebody screaming. I open my eyes and look around. Where does it come from? Who is screaming? It is my mother!

People are crowding around.

"What happened? Why did you scream?"

My mother gestures, tries to point at something. Her lips trembling, she wants to say something and can't. She sinks back onto the pillow, almost fainting.

Realising that they won't get anything out of my mother, they start looking everywhere - in the closet, under the bed, in the bed.

All of a sudden there is the sound of the nurse yelling. With a strange shrieking voice, she shouts repeatedly: "Cats! Help! Cats!"

People exchange glances, not understanding what she is saying. What does she mean? Apart from the word "cats" they can't get anything out of her either, she is so upset.

My grandmother is clearly shaken by this unexpected drama. But she pulls herself together, takes a good look around in the bed and laughing, as if to hide her own fears, she calls out, "*Mazl tov*, the cat had kittens, a good sign!"

Apparently, this is not a good sign. People are uneasy. They murmur.

"On the same day...in the same bed with cats?"

"People are born the same way as cats."

They have managed to calm my mother down. Once again, nobody has eyes for me. My mother falls asleep. And with that, the first day has come to an end. I am, thank God, one day old, and I have already gone through quite a lot.

The third day following my birth is the Sabbath. Some big, red-faced Gentile woman has put me in the bath this time. I am not so afraid anymore because I already know what is happening.

I am lying in bed with my mother. She looks at me with even greater tenderness than yesterday. I open my eyes, wanting to have another look at the new world. I am already used to the darkness. Suddenly it becomes even darker than before.

A group of women have come in, taking over the alcove. I look at them. They say something, make hand gestures, take me in their arms, pass me around like a precious object. They smile at my mother and me. In the meantime, my grandmother has come in with a tray full of cakes and liqueurs.

The women make her plead, pretending not to want to taste any of the treats - the preserves, the cherry brandy, berry juice and honey wine - but eventually, when my grandmother doesn't give in, they open their little beaks and are willing to eat something for her sake.

Men also stick their heads into the women's alcove. They talk, their faces contorted from frowning, with their hands waving in the air and their beards trembling with excitement. They are almost having convulsions.

This time it is my father who manages to convince them, not my grandmother. I am given the name of one of his relatives, Sarah Rivke.

Now they need a wet nurse. My mother is weak and pale, with such transparent, blue-veined, narrow hands, that she can hardly lift me. As a middle-class woman, she is unable to breast-feed me. I am the opposite: a strong, healthy girl, a little guzzler. I never stop crying; all I want to do is eat.

My grandmother says that she will not give me to a Gentile wet nurse, if she can help it. She cannot find a Jewish one. The chemist claims that if I get used to powdered milk, it will be better than my mother's milk. I, however, make it clear that I don't want to get used to powdered milk, and I throw up all the time.

It is all rather difficult! My grandmother is upset. My mother even more so. But my father comforts them by saying that surely the Lord will help them. And He does.

One of our neighbours has remembered that she knows this wet nurse, and she has brought her to us. She is called Reyzl. Her voice is that of a soldier, and she has two red eyes, which scare me. She will not come to our house; she has six children of her own. But she has no choice.

Everything is arranged. She receives a deposit.

Reyzl lifts me out of the cradle. She takes out a big, white breast, which looks like a piece of risen dough, and gives it to me to suck, to see if I like it. Well, what can I tell you? I almost drown with pleasure. I sense the taste of a good wet nurse.

Reyzl looks from one to the other happily.

"Well, what do you have to say?"

My mother and grandmother glance at each other furtively and keep silent.

Now I have the good fortune to be living with Reyzl. Not that she really needs anyone else around - they are living in a room the size of a large cupboard. When Reyzl brings me home, her husband comes to welcome me, carrying their smallest child in his arms with the other five heirs swarming around him. He looks extremely pleased with my arrival.

"Now, what do you say to that, eh?" beams Reyzl. "Ten zlotys a week, upon my word as an honest Jewish woman! Plus old clothes and shoes. On top of that they will give all their repair work just to you from now on! Do you hear me, Beyrish?"

Beyrish remains silent. He has turned away so that his breadwinner will not see his delight.

"She is more of a man than I am, I swear. She earns a zloty faster," he thinks to himself. But he pulls himself together immediately. "Where are we going to put the cradle?" They think about it for a long time.

Then Reyzl's husband, who is a master at rearranging all the things in his tiny home, hits his wrinkled, low forehead with his hard hand and calls out cheerfully: "Reyzl, I've got it! Under the table!"

To cut a long story short, I was shoved under the table in my little cradle.

My eyes wide open I stare in amazement at the table's filthy underside, which is covered all over with spider webs, and I think with sadness, "This is the new world I have tumbled into? And this is its heaven?"

I weep bitter tears.

# A Silk Gabardine

The Gliskers had lived in the village for a very long time. Yidel Glisker had inherited a shop, which supplied all the needs both of the village and the surrounding countryside. He ran it single-handedly. He was a tall, broad-shouldered Jew, more than capable of looking after himself. The peasants held him in the highest esteem.

He would allow his wife to help him in the shop, except for those times when he had to leave the village to buy new stock.

"A Jewish woman," Yidel claimed, "is responsible for the home and the children. That's best for everyone."

Rochel, his wife, did not agree. But she knew only too well that if Yidel said no, it meant no, and she preferred not to argue. So she set up her own business, a dairy farm.

Yidel let her get on with it. As long as she did not interfere in his affairs, he raised no objections. On the contrary, he was pleased because it gave the womenfolk something to do. He even went so far as to help her pick a few head of cattle. He paid the farmers and went drinking with them afterwards to celebrate striking the bargain.

Rochel was as good at business as Yidel. Like her husband, she refused to depend on anyone else. She did everything - she milked the cows, heated the basins of sour milk, lifted the heavy stones onto the cheeses and churned the butter. She even sewed the cheese bags herself.

The only thing her daughters did was to tend the cows grazing in the meadows as they sought the longest and lushest grass. When the cows returned in the evening, their udders were ready to burst. Rochel would then squat with a sense of deep satisfaction on the three-legged milking stool. She pulled the brownish pink teats with her strong fingers until the udders started to become longer. She would then quickly move her stool and the pail to relieve the next cow.

The cows licked her hands with their moist tongues. It was their way of thanking her.

The warm milk in the pails and the smell of manure in the shed made Rochel feel strong. At moments like these, she felt able to move mountains.

As for her daughters, who always spent the whole summer in the open air, caressed by the warm sunlight, they grew up tall and slender, like the pine trees in the neighbouring forest.

Visiting Jews from the surrounding villages, who drove up in their rickety little carts drawn by emaciated horses, to buy milk and butter and the enormous cheeses, could not help noticing all this. These Jews dared not venture near Rochel's shed out of fear of being thrown in the air by a cow and they were angered at seeing the Glisker girls grow up doing the kind of work non-Jewish girls did. It wasn't done! And Yidel himself was wholly engrossed in business and Rochel looked more like a sturdy peasant than a Jewish woman.

So, whenever Rochel refused to lower the price of the milk or cheese, they were quick to remind Yidel that their way of life was highly improper.

"What will become of your children, may they have long and happy lives. How come that a Jew like yourself, Reb Yidel, allows his daughters to grow up in the fields? What are they, *shikses*? You can't have it both ways. You will never be able to make a match! What is all this? It is completely unheard of for a fine Jew like yourself, Reb Yidel, to have his Jewish children looking after cattle, especially your children, Reb Yidel!"

Yidel could not have cared less. The only effect their words had on him was that he felt like grabbing his wife's customers by their scrawny necks and giving them a good shake, so that they would never again feel the desire to poke their noses into other people's affairs.

He knew perfectly well they did not mean a word they said. They were angry because his wife refused to give her goods away at half price, while they themselves had no qualms whatsoever about charging the poor women in the *shtetl*, the little town where most of the Jews lived, twice as much for a pint of milk or a few ounces of butter. That was the reason they said those things. They were envious of his prosperity, may no harm come to him. And so Yidel paid them no heed.

But then something happened. One evening he chanced upon his eldest daughter Royze locked in an embrace with a non-Jewish lad, lying out in the open fields. They lay there just like animals, it was a forbidden liaison; it couldn't be allowed!

After this encounter, Yidel no longer ridiculed the small-minded Jews and their endless comments. On the contrary, he listened to them attentively, pondering and brooding over every word they said. And towards the end of summer, instead of preparing themselves to drive into the nearby town for the High Holidays as mere visitors, the Gliskers sold their secluded cottage. They loaded all their merchandise onto spacious carts, and roped the cattle up behind them. They packed themselves off to the *shtetl* for good.

After they had settled on the other side of the forest, Yidel gradually remembered all the stories he had once been told about village Jews; how their children would mingle with non-Jewish boys and girls, get a bit too friendly with them, and bring shame upon their parents.

As he was having these thoughts, his heart went out to the respectable town Jews who were his new neighbours. For the first time he felt some real affinity with them. He looked at them in a way which was very different from before, when these same people had come to his place to buy wood from him. He even regarded his wife's old customers differently. He noticed how some of them sat in the small synagogue every evening, and studied what, he did not know. He soon found out, through the *shammes*, the rabbi's assistant, that one of them, the fellow with the scrawny neck, was well ahead of the others, and was working hard - on a chapter of the *Mishna*.

Yidel would peep furtively over their shoulders, and to his dismay he found that not only did he not understand a single word, he could not even read the script. A strange, new desire took hold of him. He wanted to have access to the hidden mysteries of these yellowish, well-thumbed pages of the Talmud. An idea struck him. He would hire a tutor. He would pay him whatever he asked, and more, but on one condition only: not a single soul was to know about it. On no account did he want to be thought of as a peasant.

People in the town knew that Yidel was a man of means. On the very first Sabbath following his arrival, he was called up during the synagogue service, a special honour. The *shammes* assigned him a place among the most dignified members of the community.

Life in the *shtetl* suited Yidel. His business flourished. He had found himself a teacher and he made good progress in his studies. There was one thing that really upset him, though. He was the only one at the front of the synagogue wearing a worsted gabardine. With his great height and huge back, which concealed half a dozen other worshippers, he looked inappropriately dressed in that woollen coat. There he was, in the easternmost section of the synagogue, surrounded by silk and satin. He felt completely out of place.

On the face of it, it seemed simple enough. He could certainly afford a new coat, praise be to God. All he had to do was order a few yards of silk and send for Fishel, the tailor, and that would be that.

As it turned out, Yidel, the man for whom nothing in the world was too difficult, was unable to get himself a silk gabardine.

So, every Sabbath, after the service had ended, Yidel would pace up and down the front aisle of the synagogue nervously, unsure where to put his big, clumsy feet. Softly he repeated in a wistful sing-song voice, half to himself, half to the people around him who were all clad in silk and satin:

"*Gut Shabbes! Oy, Gut Shabbes, Gut Shabbes,* May you have a good Sabbath!"

On one occasion Yidel's eccentric behaviour brought a smile to the face of one of his fellow worshippers. The man muttered something into his distinguished beard and snorted out an incomprehensible comment, hinting at the vulgarity of Yidel's conduct; the way he circled the small synagogue, his work-worn hands folded behind him, a spotted red handkerchief clutched between his massive fingers.

One boy of about thirteen, Simcha, the Talmud master's youngest son, was quicker than the grown-ups to understand what this fine Jew, Reb Mordechai, was getting at with that delicate twitch of his nose. And so Simcha started pacing up and down as well, his own skinny body hiding behind Yidel's broad shoulders, and with a roguish smile he chanted softly:

"*Gut Shabbes! Gut shabbes!* Soon we will enjoy have the traditional *Shabbes* meal, *grobe kishke* and a *cholent* stew!"

Yidel folded up his prayer shawl and handed it over to the *shammes*. As soon as he had left the synagogue, everybody burst out laughing; nevertheless they reprimanded Simcha: "Shame on you, little rascal! Making fun of a Jew, on *Shabbes* no less!"

Little did they know that Simcha was Yidel's tutor, and that once a week he went over to Yidel to help him read a chapter of the Torah, for which Yidel paid him two zlotys. Every Sabbath afternoon, Simcha would make his way secretly through a fresh layer of blue-white snow. It required some effort to get to the house, which was located at the far end of the *shtetl*. It stood there submerged either in snow and sunlight or in snow and mud, depending on what day it was, eagerly awaiting the guest.

Every Sabbath he would find Yidel upright in bed, looking wide awake and rested. He bossed his middle daughter Fayge around in a fatherly fashion.

"I say, Faytshe, hand me a glass of water, will you. And make sure it is cr-r-rystal clear-r - I don't want any wor-rms in it!"

His emphasis on these words invariably tickled Simcha. They conjured up two images: one, the flashing crystal shine of running water; the other, a stagnant pool full of wriggling worms. When Fayge appeared again with a glass of ordinary water, he felt cheated by father and daughter alike, and spitefully he imitated Yidel under his breath, rolling his tongue: "I say, Faytshe, cr-r-rystal clear-r-r, and no wor-rms!"

But Yidel was blissfully unaware of Simcha's clowning; the peacefulness of the Sabbath had taken hold of him completely. The boy watched him drinking and scrutinising the glass after every sip, to make sure there were no worms. When Yidel had finished his glass, he put it on the floor. He wiped a few glistening drops which had settled in his beard with the edge of the bedsheet and only then would he become aware of Simcha's presence.

"Ah, Simchale, *Gut Shabbes*!" He was always pleased to see him. Cheerfully he would call to his wife: "Rochel, time to get up! He's here already!"

On the opposite side of the room there was another carved bed, an exact replica of Yidel's, and Rochel lay there fully dressed, her feet resting on a three-legged milking stool. She was very nearly as tall as Yidel, and almost as sturdily built. She was wearing a white, linen blouse and a red, check skirt. With a red and yellow kerchief tied around her head and a string of scarlet beads around her neck, she certainly looked like one of the peasant women who came to the *shtetl* on Sundays.

Yidel's words made her stir in her sleep, and she turned around in the bed. The little stool started moving with her. It tumbled slowly towards the edge of the bed, only just clinging to the heels of her shoes, until it finally landed on the floor with a big thump. This really woke her up. Struggling to balance her large body, she sat upright and smiled respectfully at the young scholar: "Ah, Reb Simchale!"

"*Gut Shabbes!*" Simcha tried with all his might not to look at her. Still, from the corner of his eye he could make out that the red headscarf had slid down somewhat, revealing her hair; real, shining, black hair with a wide, pale parting in the middle - something he had never seen with any of the other Jewish women in the *shtetl*. Simcha was shocked. It was the same almost every Sabbath; but she never seemed to notice that anyone could see her real hair.

And it was not only little Simcha who wondered. The whole *shtetl* was mystified. Nobody understood the Gliskers; they were clearly Jews, pious Jews even, but at the same time they were different from everybody else. No other Jews behaved the way they did.

It was completely unheard of: Jews that were healthier than Gentiles; it was unnatural to have daughters as tall as trees, large-breasted giants with enormous shoulders and brightly sparkling eyes. It was simply too much! The mother was just as tall, just as strong, and fit, and her eyes were shining just as brightly as those of her daughters. The amount of work these women took on was incredible!

After they had settled in the *shtetl*, Rochel had taken charge of Yidel's business. Week in, week out she stood behind her counter selling a seemingly endless supply of herrings. The peasants did not want to buy anywhere else. It was all "Rochele this" and "Rochele that". It was hard to say why they all liked her so much, except maybe - may God not punish me for these words - for the fact that she looked like one of them. Oh dear! Rochel herself did not pay much attention to her customers, except when a peasant wife crushed the herring while looking for roe or when some old crone tried to slip a fish into her bosom. She weighed the merchandise on the green scales. She lifted the large bags of salt with such ease one would have thought they contained feathers instead of heavy crystals. She even rolled big barrels of petrol and oil over the greasy, black shop floor, as swiftly as if they were empty, and if one of them got stuck behind a loose floorboard, she simply lifted the barrel over her shoulder and that was that!

Since everybody preferred to buy from Rochel, the other tradeswomen might as well have closed up shop. They sat there idly, with nothing to do the whole day but wallow in their misery. The floors of their shops dried out; the herring in their barrels turned soft; the rest of their stock went putrid and their herring barrels rusted. The salt shrank in their bags. Even the oil barrels seemed to dry out. With each passing day, the envy and bitterness of the shopkeepers grew greater.

The Gliskers, for their part, kept getting richer. Their shop was bursting with merchandise. There was not one single empty shelf. Sabbath meals at Yidel's home became ever grander, and the naps afterwards longer. The fruit and sweets with which they treated Simcha were more delicious than ever before.

Rochel got up and smoothed out the blanket. She then went out to freshen herself up after her rest.

Yidel had stumbled out of bed in the meantime. He put on his clothes and followed his wife into the other room. Devoyre, the youngest of the girls, who was twelve but had the looks of a twenty-year-old, arranged her father's bedding. She made it just as smooth as her mother would have done. Yidel stretched himself out, and removed a few small feathers, which had crept into his beard, while he'd been asleep. He rolled them into tiny balls and shot them across the room. He smiled at Simcha. They both took a seat at the table.

"I say, Simcha, how many yards of silk do you reckon I'd need for a new gabardine? Hmmm, what do you think?" he asked the boy as if he were a tailor.

Simcha glanced at Yidel as though to measure him. It struck him that the man might easily need thirty yards.

"Well, I should say about fifteen," Simcha blurted out, and he blushed fiercely.

Yidel did not reply. He already regretted having asked the question;

he felt ill at ease, as if he had made a fool of himself. He quickly got up and walked to the bookcase, where he took out a *chumash* containing the five books of Moses, bound in calf with large golden lettering on the embossed spine. Turning to the weekly Torah portion, he respectfully carried the open book to the table as if it were of great importance.

Yidel sat at the head of the table with Simcha at his right side and Devoyre opposite him. Her elbows planted firmly on the table and her fists embedded in her fleshy cheeks, she did not take her eyes off Simcha for a moment.

Simcha pretended not to notice her presence. His thin forefinger began to flow along the printed lines.

"'*Vayaitsa Yakov mibeer Shiba*', which means - And Jacob went out from Beersheba, '*Vayelich Charana*', and went towards Charan."

The meaning of the sentence was simple enough, thought Yidel. Jacob had left Beersheba, just as he, Yidel, had moved away from Bojonitz. But what he could not manage to figure out, was the meaning of the individual words. He was too ashamed to ask. He got more and more confused as he blundered his way through, much to the dismay of his young teacher, who tried to make him understand each word. Tirelessly Simcha explained everything, over and over again, like a born teacher.

Yidel bore it patiently. He kept trying until he finally got it. His face beamed. Simcha was so delighted that he forgot his earlier reserve and looked at the girl triumphantly.

Devoyre's large grey eyes stared back at him, not understanding why these two were so happy all of a sudden. She was mystified as to why her father, who was such an important man, would allow a little boy to teach him a lesson.

In the meantime, Rochel had come in with a large tray of sweetmeats. Even though Simcha was sitting with his back to it, he could feel its presence, and it spurred him on. His thin forefinger danced across the page now:

"And Jacob went out from Beersheba..."

"Well, well!" Yidel rubbed his hands contentedly. "It's time to have a bite," he said, and he placed the bookmark back on the page. Rochel carried the book, with great reverence, to the bed where she placed it carefully on the green blanket, as if it were a weak, sickly child. Then she started to hand out the sweetmeats.

"Eat, Simchale! Don't be ashamed! As it is written in the *Ethics of the Fathers...* Uh..." Yidel was lost for words. "Hmmm? What does it say there again?" Yidel wrinkled his forehead as if he expected to find the answer there. Simcha quickly helped him out: "Where there is no food there is no Torah."

"Exactly." Yidel remembered the phrase now, and he offered Simcha a poppy-seed cake: "Eat, and I hope you'll enjoy it!" Yidel radiated contentment as he himself dug into the delicacies his wife was offering.

"Reb Simchale should eat more," Rochel said while she placed an enormous piece of strudel in front of him. "Please, you must have some of these as well," she added, pushing a plate with almond biscuits in his direction and pouring tea at the same time.

That winter Yidel would go straight after his Sabbath lesson to the synagogue with Simcha. Rather, he would go first and Simcha would follow a few moments later, on his own, as if he had nothing to do with Yidel. Darkness came early in those months; there was hardly enough time for Rochel to stumble through the prayers she had to recite at the close of the Sabbath.

When Yidel returned from the evening service, he found the fire already glowing. A gigantic iron kettle with potato peelings for the animals was boiling in the kitchen. Next to it stood another pot, not much smaller, with potatoes for the family. The red, bubbling mass of beetroot soup filled the house with its sour smell.

Rochel hastily mixed the food for the chickens, which flew impatiently down from their shelves behind the beds. They circled around her like angry devils. It did not take long for a cackle to erupt among the birds, picking madly at the food and at each other, stealing bits out of each other's beaks, although there was easily enough for all of them. At times, the battle became so fierce that some even lost a few feathers, but when Rochel scolded them, they immediately started to eat more quietly, as if they realised that their mistress was right.

The livestock in the stall were getting impatient too. Especially Rochel's favourite. All her cows were good-looking, but this one was supreme, a real beauty! Rochel had raised her single-handedly. She had bought her as a small calf and raised her like a princess. The cow was brown with white, shining patches, which gave her extra charm. Her udders were also different from the other cows; not miserable flabby things, but healthy udders, bursting with thick, creamy milk. It took all of Rochel's strength to milk her!

Those Saturday nights were more than even Rochel could cope with, and she had to ask her daughter for help: "Feyge, add some wood to the fire! The potato skins aren't boiling! Feyge, you are crushing her udder. Not like that, Feyge, you silly girl!"

But Feyge was hardly ever there on Saturday evening. She usually slipped away right after they had finished the stew and she did not come back until long after *havdalah*. Things were even worse when Yidel took it into his head to drive to town overnight to replenish his stocks. Then Rochel not only had to deal with the chickens and the cows, but she also had to prepare a meal for Yidel before he went off on his trip, and she did not know which mouth to feed first.

At such moments, Rochel would get flustered and she would no longer be able to remember the name of objects or people. Everything became "thingamy" - the cow, the horse, the chickens, her husband, her daughters. They were all referred to by one single name: "thingamy".

"Yidel, have you already given thingamy to the thingamy?" What she meant was: "Yidel, have you already given hay to the horse?"

"Yidel, don't forget to take the thingamy!" In other words, "Yidel, don't forget to take the piece of paper!"

"Thingamy, the thingamies will get thingamied!" This was Rochel's way of saying: "Feyge, the potatoes will get boiled to pieces!" It was one of Rochel's weaknesses to think that, as soon as she had put on a pot of potatoes, they were already overdone.

Yidel studied long and hard with the help of Simcha, until one day the local matchmaker, who knew everybody's secrets, decided the time had come to match Yidel with Reb Isaac, the Talmud master. And so, in due course a marriage was arranged between Royze, Yidel's eldest daughter, and Menasseh, who was Simcha's sixteen-year-old brother.

As soon as Royze was betrothed, Rochel had to stop ordering her around. It so happened that Yidel had decided that his daughter was in fact a delicate creature, and she had to be spared. No more rough jobs for Royze he warned his wife. Besides, as a future daughter-in-law of the Talmud master, she'd have plenty of dainty work to keep her busy!

And so Royze sat whole days tracing monograms on pillowcases for herself and for her husband-to-be. (Needless to say it was Yidel who provided everything for both parties.) She crocheted, for herself and for her future father-in-law, matzo-bags for the unleavened bread that they would eat at the Passover. She sewed covers for the *challah*, the braided bread for the Sabbath, and embroidered a *tallis* bag for her betrothed's prayer shawl. She toiled over endless quantities of linen and even made an apron for her future mother-in-law. Royze laboured and Yidel paid, since Reb Isaac, the Talmud master, was a most learned man, a most particular man, a most irascible man and...a hopelessly penniless one.

It had not been easy to convince Royze she was now a fragile flower, because she loved to be hale and hearty, as indeed she was. There was nothing she liked more than hard work. Except maybe the long Sabbath afternoons and the ensuing Saturday evenings, when she should have been at home helping her mother, but hardly ever was, since it was so hard to tear herself apart from her village sweetheart. She detested doing needlework and pricking her fingers. She hated having to dress up like a doll and walk carefully around the house. She hated behaving like a lady. What she hated most of all, was Menasseh, her future husband. But gradually she got used to the idea (or so it seemed). She admitted that she was a different person now, and there was no way her mother could order her around anymore.

Rochel had no choice but to work like a dog - especially during the long winter evenings following the Sabbath. In summer, when the days were longer, Sabbath lasted the whole day, thankfully. Then she just had to wait for Yidel to come home and make *havdalah*. She would recite the *Shema* for the last time in the day - and hop into bed! In summer there were no potato peelings to be cooked after Sabbath, no chickens to be fed. The cows were satisfied; the meadows were there for them to graze on just as they pleased. The chickens happily scraped around outside the whole day, laying their eggs amidst the wooden boards. Rochel hardly saw them. Yidel would stay in at night and life was good.

Yidel also preferred the Sabbaths in summer, although he did not mind the other ones as much as his wife. His affairs had prospered exceedingly in his new home. His stock of timber had multiplied, so that it took up more and more space behind the spacious wooden cottage. The cows now had to graze in fields much further away from the house because of it.

In summer, Yidel did not accompany Simcha to the synagogue, because the evening prayers were taking place much later. But Yidel could not renounce the pleasures of the Sabbath.

He decided to send Simcha home, and stroll around amidst his piles of timber, while measuring them with his eye.

He knew it was forbidden to measure on the Sabbath. Therefore he measured only with his eye, which gave him great satisfaction. Soon there would not be a single empty patch of grass left. The cows were hidden from view already! The piles of wood had almost driven the animals into the lake. It was not a bad thing, thought Yidel, since the grass was lusher over there. But why was it forbidden to count? The question kept nagging at him. He felt a sudden urge to count the various kinds of wood he had in stock: pine, alder, and birch. The desire was so strong that he quickly clasped both hands behind his back and walked in the direction of the cows in order not to give in to the temptation. Without knowing it, the cows had saved him from a sin.

He noticed that the grass was indeed good next to the lake. The cows were begging to be relieved, though. The Sabbath dragged on, and Yidel felt pity for the cows and their bursting udders. There was nothing he could do, and he walked back to the wood. That wood was worth a fortune, may no harm come to it, he thought as he squeezed himself between the piles.

Yidel loved the wood. What he liked about it was its smell. Especially on a hot day, when the resin became soft and trickled along the trunks like honey. The fragrance was so delicious that he was tempted to scrape it off the tree.

Yidel was only human. Although he tried very hard not to, he occasionally touched one of the cows, or counted a few pieces of wood. And who knows, maybe that was allowed after all?

On the one hand, he would like to ask the rabbi's advice. On the other hand,  however, he could just tell what his reaction would be. The rabbi would be shocked: How could a Jew not know something so basic, that one was not allowed to count wood on the Sabbath? Counting by mouth, that was forbidden too! And using only your eyes, yes, that too was a sin of course! That's what the rabbi would say. He might smile in a friendly fashion at him, but deep in his heart he would mock him for such a foolish question. Even a child would know the answer, and the rabbi would regard him as a peasant.

Yidel sighed deeply and turned around to the path that led to the synagogue. The chickens followed him, as if they recognised him. Yidel hated it. He chased them away with the yellow and red handkerchief: "Shoo! Shoo!"

He looked around and saw they were still there: "Shoo! Shoo!"

He hated looking like a peasant. And, of course, just at that moment, Borechl Keppel showed up. They bumped into each other almost every week, since Borechl liked to go for a summer walk through Yidel's wood, to inhale the sweet fragrance of the pine resin and to look at the clear blue sky.

"*Gut Shabbes*, Reb Yidel," Borechl said, and a small, hairy hand appeared out of a paper cuff. Dark, glistening eyes smiled at Yidel. Borechl had a smallish head. His moist, black hair hung onto the paper collar around his neck. It was hard to distinguish the beard from the hair on his neck.

"*Gut Shabbes! Gut Shabbes!*" Yidel grabbed Borechl's shrivelled little hand with his own enormous fist, in which it disappeared completely, and he gave it a friendly shake, which made Borechl jump in the air.

"Aaaaahh! How are you doing, Reb Yidel?" Borechl tried to extricate his crushed fingers from Yidel's iron clasp.

"Fine, praise be to the Almighty!"

"When will the marriage, God willing, take place, Reb Yidel?"

"Why do you ask?" The question surprised Yidel.

"Just like that, for no special reason! A good friend is interested in these matters."

"Nothing has been agreed yet, but I reckon it's going to be on the *Shabbes* after the fast of Av, God willing," Yidel replied, and both men walked to the synagogue to attend the evening prayers.

Together they strode along the meadow, which was patchy and dry where the piles of wood had left their mark. Furthermore, in many places, the grass had been ripped out by its roots. The earth seemed to be wounded.

Yidel's shadow was gliding across the grass like a giant. Borechl noticed how insignificant his own shadow looked as it danced alongside that of Yidel, pursuing the mighty figure moving through the empty landscape.

He did not even reach Yidel's shoulders.

Borechl tumbled down the ladder of his own self-esteem when he realised how tiny he looked next to Yidel. Desperately he tried to make himself taller, by walking on his toes. He did not stop talking for a minute, gesticulating wildly with his small hands, so that his alter ego on the grass made odd, grand gestures, and he sweated.

Thus they had walked almost every Sabbath together to the evening service. And every week Yidel was perturbed because he did not dare to ask Borechl about the issue of counting wood on the Sabbath. It would have answered his question once and for all, but he did not have the courage. And every week Borechl was depressed because of his own pathetic size.

That day Yidel was distressed about something else as well. When they passed the synagogue alley, he had heard the women, who met every Sabbath for a chat on the bench in front of Chane-Rochel's house, gossiping about him and his family.

"So, I am asking you, does a Jew look like that? If he was really a Jew, would he live the way he does? Jews aren't supposed to be so lucky. And then I'm not even talking about 'them'! Have you ever seen Jewish daughters as healthy as *shikses*? Or a *yidene* who kisses her cows? May hair grow on the palm of my hand, if they are Jews!" Chane-Rochel exclaimed, as if this was definitive proof that the Gliskers were not in fact Jews, but converted peasants.

The sun was still high in the sky when Borechl and Yidel entered the synagogue that day.

"*Gut Shabbes*, Reb Yidel!" The rabbi himself came up to him.

The little synagogue was steeped in sunlight. Golden motes of sunlight were pouring in through the closed window, dancing on the *bime*, the raised platform from where the prayers were said, and ending with a glitter of splendour on the menorah. The sight filled Yidel's heart with joy, and all his earlier worries disappeared instantly, like clouds melting in a sudden burst of hot sunshine.

"*Gut Shabbes! Gut Shabbes! Gut Shabbes! Gut Shabbes!*" Yidel burst out in endless greetings. He was overjoyed by the honour bestowed on him by no less a person than the rabbi, and by the sight of the sunshine resting on the menorah which he himself had recently donated. A piece of solid silver, it stood there on the *bime*. No wonder the golden sunlight was attracted by it, he thought.

Thus Yidel lived surrounded by riches and honour. Everything he touched became a success. Even his lessons with Simcha started to pay off, and every Sabbath Simcha was a little more satisfied with him.

The moment had come. Yidel's large front room was bare of all furniture, except for long wooden benches lining the walls. A large paraffin lamp hung from the centre of the ceiling. Smaller lamps, which looked like Chinese lanterns, had been suspended across the freshly whitewashed room. The walls were draped with colourful paper ribbons, plain and curled, coiled or crimped - a dazzling mixture of green, red, yellow and orange! The floor was strewn with fine, light-coloured sand.

Rochel was not wearing her usual red headscarf, but a black shiny wig, which had been combed up high. It was not fastened at the side by a white silk bow, such as she normally wore on Rosh Hashonah.

Yidel was clad in a new, silk gabardine. In honour of his daughter's marriage to the son of the Talmud master, he had finally made the transition to silk. His old woollen coat had been discarded for good. The sheen of the material looked magnificent on his imposing body and was only matched by the glow of his rosy, peasant cheeks. Linking himself to such a fine young man with a fine family had given him the strength to assert himself, and indeed, the new coat suited him well. It rested comfortably on his broad shoulders and it exuded an air of joy - honestly, it was as if the silk gabardine itself was rejoicing.

Rochel was helping a hired woman to arrange the cake on the trays, as well as the other delicacies. Today she called everything by its proper name; not once did she revert to "thingamy". Feyge and Devoyre were dressed in yellow embroidered dresses trimmed with endless frills and they had white ribbons in their hair.

The bride, all dressed in white, sat on an upholstered armchair, her feet resting on a little stool.

The guests were beginning to arrive. First were the village maidens, their faces reddened by hard washing, bodies tightly laced in starched fabric, in the company of their pious mothers who smelled of honey and vinegar.

The musicians were about to start playing: Gimpel with his fiddle, Hersh-Layb with his bass and Dovidl with his flute.

The bridegroom would arrive any minute. He would be accompanied by the most notable young men of the *shtetl* and by fellow students from his faraway *yeshiva*, the rabbinical academy. Simcha would walk in their midst, since he was over thirteen and considered a man now.

Yidel was so happy he could not stand still. He kept walking in and out of the rooms. He paused for a moment in front of the laden tables. He turned the paraffin lamp full on again, to reassure himself that the wick was not smoking. Then he took out his handkerchief to wipe the place of honour, where the bridegroom would soon be seated. Finally, he went into the women's room, to have another look at the bride.

What was going on? The bride sat squirming on her chair like a worm and she softly groaned into her white veil. Nobody had noticed anything, it seemed. The women showered her with kisses and blessings, they suffocated her with their embraces, drowning her pitiful, muffled moans. The girls kissed her too and wished her well, but they were more interested in the white frock, the long veil over her head, the elegant little shoes on her feet. They did not see how the bride's face was distorted in agony, changing rapidly from deathly pale to green. And now the orchestra had started up, accompanied by loud shouts:

"*Mazl tov!* Congratulations! Here comes the bridegroom! Play us a merry tune! Here comes the bridegroom!"

Women were clapping their hands:

"Here he comes! Here he comes! He has arrived!"

"May happiness be theirs their whole lives long!"

Yidel left Royze writhing on her armchair and hastened forward to meet the bridegroom, who had only just crossed the threshold. He was a pale, skinny young man, not much taller than his younger brother Simcha, and with exactly the same pointed nose. He stood in the corridor, surrounded by a cluster of young men who were all wrapped in silk, just like himself. Music filled the house.

Royze was bent double. She saw through the open door how her future husband was led through the hall. A wisp of a man, just like a doll, she thought, a silk doll.

She was seized by pity and rage at the same time. An insane urge to laugh welled up inside her. But a pain deep within her belly overwhelmed all other feelings. She wailed out loud. The women instantly surrounded her. A great uproar broke out. The bride kicked her feet in agony. She was crying like a little girl. Chane-Rochel started weeping too. Rochel kept asking for a "thingamy", completely forgetting there was no such thing as a doctor in the *shtetl*. The bridegroom, scared to death, was quickly hustled into another room. The other young men stared at him, grinning stupidly, not knowing what to say.

Somebody ordered the musicians to play as loudly as they could.

The wife of the Talmud master was so distressed that suddenly, while absent-mindedly pulling at a lock of hair, she tugged her wig off. Bald-headed, she stood there amidst the bewildered guests.

The only person who did not lose his head was Yidel. As he watched his daughter, a terrible suspicion entered his mind, so terrible that he would have been glad to see the accursed house crash down on him, his family, and all the damned guests as well.

The rabbi suggested that the bride be put to bed, to treat her with compresses and to proceed with the ceremony at her bedside. By doing so, the bride, would with God's help, soon recover.

At that moment, the Talmud master started to scream.

Yidel did not listen to the rabbi, nor to the Talmud master. Instead, still wearing his silk gabardine, he stormed into the stable, brought out two strong black horses, hitched them up, wrapped his daughter in a white eiderdown which he had grabbed from the bridal bed and carried her outside like a child. He bundled her into the cart and before Rochel had the chance to realise what he was doing and to jump in with him, Yidel had climbed up on to the seat. He cracked his whip and was off in the direction of the forest.

A deadly silence filled the house. All eyes were on the cart and its strange load. Yidel, his silken back gleaming in the twilight, whipped the horses as if he were possessed. For a short while, the cart was shrouded in a cloud of dust, and then it was gone. The forest stood motionless in the distance as it always did.

The forest was inhabited by dark forces. Nobody in the *shtetl* doubted this. In summer witches skimmed over treetops on their brooms and in winter they appeared in the guise of wild wolves.

Strange stories were told about that forest. But none as strange as the news Yidel brought with him, after a mere half hour's stay there.

A whirlwind of dust announced the return of Yidel's cart. Immediately, the racket in the house died down and it was replaced by an expectant hush. Evil tongues were silenced by this sudden development.

Royze was sitting in front next to her father. Her cheeks had regained their colour. She got out of the cart by herself, without any help.

"The wedding is off!" Yidel said unceremoniously to Reb Isaac.

The tumult caused by these four words was such that no one after-wards remembered quite what had happened. One thing everybody was agreed on, though: the forest clearly had a hand in this. The dark forces had whispered in Yidel's ear, and there was no doubt that they were behind the horrible sin, which he had committed on his daughter's very wedding day.

The only one who could have told them what had taken place in the forest, was Yidel himself. Only he knew about the tree on which he had meant to hang himself; that is, before he learned from Royze that his terrible suspicion had been unfounded. But he did not say a word to anyone. When she heard him breaking down in tears and laughter at the same time, Rochel was convinced her husband had lost his mind.

That same night, after Yidel had finally managed to get rid of the last guests, he locked the front door. Then he threw off his silk gabardine and put his old woollen self back on again. The family ate their supper out of simple clay bowls, just like in the old days before they moved into the *shtetl*.

And to this day Yidel's silk gabardine lies forgotten in the attic, on top of a pile of useless junk. Every day, at dusk, it briefly catches a beam of coppery sunlight. It lies there wrapped up and motionless, underneath a layer of golden dust, like the relic of a long-lost dream.

# Reb Meyerl

That evening Reb Meyerl came home upset. The rabbinical courtroom was cloaked in sombre shadows. A lamp, standing on the large brown table, cast its light on holy books and manuscripts. They lay there, as usual, waiting for him to have something to eat and to start studying.

But Reb Meyerl was completely oblivious to the world around him. He had simply forgotten that today was Monday and that, as an observant Jew, he had been fasting the whole day. He was unaware of himself sitting there with both hands in the pockets of his heavy fur coat, staring aimlessly into the dark. He had not even heard Menasseh, his assistant, ask him three times whether he could bring in supper. Eventually Menasseh had sent for the rabbi's wife.

Reb Meyerl stood up and took off his fur coat. A puddle of water had formed on the floor near him, coming from the ice clinging to his shoes. Only now did he take off the high fur cap he had been wearing and replace it with a velvet yarmulke, his usual skullcap. Then he sat down in a carved wooden chair at the head of the table, and started to study and write.

It was so quiet in the room that one could clearly hear the scratching of the pen with which Reb Meyerl wrote down his thoughts. He wrote something down, crossed it out, wrote something else, and crossed that out as well. He was not getting anywhere. He got up and stretched himself to his full height. He almost reached the ceiling. He took down a book from the shelves.

The walls were covered with religious books - all kinds of books, precious old first editions, bound in rough leather with broad spines worn thin from piety - Talmudic tracts, works of the prophets and all the holy writings he could muster. He had everything in several copies. Some of them belonged to his father-in-law, with whom he lived even though he was rabbi of the *shtetl*; some he had received as wedding gifts. Next to the thickly bound volumes stood all sorts of smaller books by contemporary rabbis and other Jewish scholars, who had written new interpretations of the Law. Like little children, these books huddled close to the good and serious adults, who seemed so solid and wise.

He was looking for something, checking it and checking it again, but he could not find the passage that would give him real insight into the problem that was troubling him. It was impossible to solve it that day. Finally he placed his handkerchief on the book, folded a sheet in his manuscript and began to pace up and down the courtroom. His shadow followed him around, one moment spreading itself onto the walls, the next stretching out to the size of a giant on the floor, only to become strangely fat and squat a moment later.

The lamp on the table did not spread any light onto the rest of the room, which was covered in darkness. In the end, he sat down again at the head of the table. He thrust his big brown hands into his sleeves and gave up.

He realised that the evening was now lost, and that he would not learn anything that day, let alone succeed in writing any of it down. His deep, dark eyes were shining. His cheeks, which had looked crimson earlier on when he was on his way home from the synagogue in the clear, frosty night, now seemed dull brown, almost yellow. Wrinkles covered his high, young forehead, as if he were an old man.

His wife had been standing next to the table for quite a while. Only then did he notice her.

If not for the wide, pleated dress and the silk jacket trimmed with a mass of black velvet, and the yellow silk headscarf, which was bound tightly around her small shaven head, one could have mistaken her for a twelve-year-old girl; she seemed so young and small, even in these old-fashioned clothes.

"You will make yourself ill. You haven't eaten anything yet. You seem to have forgotten that you have fasted the whole day." She spoke quietly and respectfully, very unlike the way in which a wife normally speaks to her husband.

"Maybe you can go and wash now?" she asked him softly, so softly that he could hardly hear. But he did get up.

"*Nu, nu*, all right then," Reb Meyerl said without even looking in her direction. She handed him a letter. While he opened it, she kept standing there for a while, waiting for him to tell her what the letter was about. But Reb Meyerl had already forgotten she was in the room. He was reading the letter, and the more he read, the more astonished he became. Apparently, the city of Pilsk wanted to appoint him as their rabbi. The letter was signed by a delegate of the synagogue council and by a number of Jewish community members.

He had read the letter once, and then twice, and he still did not understand what it meant. He knew that Pilsk was an old city, renowned for its great rabbis. Was it possible? Could it be true that the dignitaries of Pilsk wanted to receive him in their midst, to follow in the footsteps of the great rabbi, who had made the whole world tremble with his rulings? He wasn't even thirty years old! And what a coincidence that the letter should reach him tonight, when only a minute ago he had said to himself in despair that he would be glad to leave his *shtetl*, Molits, if only he could find a post elsewhere. It was simply incredible! If he had not been an opponent of the mystically inclined Hasidic Jews he would have thought it was a miracle. But it had to be Providence. There was no doubt about it. It could not have happened just like that, for no good reason, that the letter had arrived precisely this evening, on the very same day that the well-off members of his community had caused him so much trouble.

He read the letter once more and in spite of himself, a bright smile began to soften his noble features. The wrinkles disappeared from his forehead. His dark brown eyes sparkled with warmth and beauty. They looked so full of depth and wisdom; Chanele, his wife, had never seen him like this before. It was as if he had been touched by the Divine Presence. She did not understand why her husband was so happy. Especially on a day like this when, according to Menasseh, the rabbi had every reason to be sad.

Menasseh turned on the main light. Immediately the courtroom felt warm and cheerful. The parchment lampshade looked old and grey now. It did not seem to give any light. Menasseh switched it off and removed it from the table. The shadows had vanished.

Menasseh struggled in with the copper basin, together with a heavy, copper jug, and the rabbi started to wash. The water in the basin glistened like silver and seemed boiling hot.

His wife came back into the room with a servant girl behind her carrying the food. Menasseh took the tray from her at the door, and Chanele placed everything on the table with great care. A cloud of steam rose from the silver dishes, and soon a wonderful smell pervaded the whole room. But Reb Meyerl barely touched his food. He made one blessing after another and hardly ate a thing. Then he recited the final blessing and Menasseh cleared the table.

Reb Meyerl tried once again to work on his manuscript and to consult various books, but he failed to make any sense of it. It was impossible to study. His cheeks had a dark red colour again. He felt guilty towards the Jews of Molits, the rich as well as the poor ones. After all, he had grown up in this *shtetl*. It seemed to him that he had sinned against them today. While drinking his tea after supper, he remembered how he had smiled with pleasure at the letter, which he read over and over again. He looked at the shiny, scalding hot samovar, and noticed how it stood there, comfortable and cheerful, humming its familiar tune for him, Reb Meyerl, as it had done for many generations before, in this wealthy, venerable home. It suddenly dawned on him that the samovar took up too important a place: it was standing in the centre of the table, amidst his books and papers, and he told Menasseh to move the samovar to a corner.

Menasseh could not believe his ears. This was the first time he had heard the rabbi speak in such a critical way about his beloved samovar, which stood by him during every need and difficulty, but he did what the rabbi asked him to do. "He is putting everything off this evening, even his studies. He is in a dream," Menasseh said to himself. "Hmmm, evil spirits are getting a hold over him today."

Reb Meyerl was starting to feel hot. He simply did not know what to do. But then he had an idea: he would write to the dignitaries of Pilsk, offer them his apologies and stay in Molits. Yes! That's how he would atone for his sins.

He started to write straightaway. In order to formulate his own reply correctly, he read what the letter had to say one more time. Suddenly he noticed a few tiny lines that were added in the corner. He had not seen these before due to his earlier excitement: "And so, if the frost is not too bad, we will arrive, God willing, in Molits tomorrow late afternoon or early evening."

That put the whole affair in a completely different light. Now he had no choice but to receive them. It also meant that the matter had been somewhat taken out of his hands.

He kept torturing himself with all kinds of thoughts. Eventually a bright idea brought him some comfort: he would simply take a step back and leave everything to Providence.

The last thing he did was to send Menasseh to one of the council delegates of Molits with a note informing him about the contents of the letter, including the fact that the group from Pilsk was expected to come with a formal invitation. He also expressed the wish to see the delegate the following day, God willing, in order to discuss the matter with him further.

What he had not specified in his note was when exactly the delegate should come. He had done this on purpose; it was part of his resolution to rid himself of all responsibility. Providence was to make sure everything would turn out well. He would wait and see. If the official from Molits arrived before the delegation from Pilsk, then he would stay. If he did not turn up the following day, then that would be a sign that he had to go and become rabbi of Pilsk.

He started to feel somewhat lighter. It was as if Providence had taken a heavy weight off his shoulders. After all, can a human being know God's ways? Providence would run its course.

After reading the evening prayers, he went to bed early, so that he would be able to get up to recite the midnight prayers. He was so calm now that he fell asleep in less than five minutes.

It was the middle of winter, and the snow had been lying for weeks like a massive blanket, held in place by the frost. Not a single snowflake was moving. Only those who had to, ventured out on the street. Nevertheless, that afternoon the synagogue was bursting with people. The wealthy Jews had gathered there, as well as Jews who prayed alone at home most of the time and who normally only came on the Sabbath.

They all wanted to hear the latest news; they wanted to find out what the outcome of the whole affair would be. Would their rabbi, who was still only in his twenties (whom they remembered being carried into *cheder* for children's Hebrew classes, as if it were yesterday), stay on in Molits, or would the Jews from Pilsk take him away from them?

The *shtetl* was in a spin.

Come on! It was all so trivial. All the rabbi had done, long may he live, was make an effort on behalf of the poor. He had suggested that rich members of the Molits community should pay twice as much tax this winter because of the harsh weather conditions. The money would then be used to deliver a bundle of wood to those who needed it, some cooked food as well, and they would be able to donate shoes to poor boys learning Torah. What if he had scolded the wealthy a little? They deserved it! Respectable Jews! Did they really think that God had created the world for them, and them alone? As the workers discussed this, deep in their hearts they were secretly enjoying the scandal. At the same time they dreaded one possible outcome: that the poor Jews of Molits would not receive any help and that they would lose, God forbid, the rabbi, their dear rabbi, the young genius of Molits. After all, yesterday that fat pig had told the rabbi that it was his job to give his opinion on religious matters, and not to interfere in community affairs. He had added that the council members would take care of that, as the rabbi was too young and had no understanding of worldly affairs. So what if the rabbi really stepped down! He definitely didn't need the few roubles they paid him every week. He gave these away to the poor anyway. He even added some of his own and he received more money from his father-in-law for charity than from anybody else. So who knows, they said, especially now that these people from Pilsk had suddenly appeared.

The council representative was angry with the rabbi that he hadn't sent a letter to Pilsk immediately, saying that he would turn down their offer. Nevertheless he had called a meeting of the members of the Molits community (the "respectable" members only, of course). There had been a lot of talking and shouting, and still they were unable to reach an agreement: should they go to the rabbi and persuade him not to leave, or should they wait and see what he had in mind?

Some members thought it was best to go and dissuade him, and to offer their apologies. But the more affluent members, who were held in the highest esteem, did not agree. They said it was never a good thing to try and persuade anyone by begging. "If we beg him to stay, we will only make matters worse! He will drive us mad afterwards," said one of them, a complete idiot, who had a great deal of influence because he gave large amounts of money to ease the needs of the community.

The whole situation created such a stir in the *shtetl*, it was as if it were a matter of life and death.

The one who made the biggest fuss, was the rabbi's mother-in-law, Khaye Devoyre. "You will never convince me to send the child away!" she told her husband. Khaye Devoyre still referred to the rabbi's wife as "the child" because she was their only daughter and rather small at that. "I will not send the child away to a strange city. She was born here, and this is where she will stay until she's a hundred and twenty! Do you understand? And it is high time you had a wash. The food is getting as cold as ice," she said angrily.

Reb Avrom Aaron slowly washed his hands and dried them with the large, white towel. He said a blessing before the meal and smiled at his grand-child, who was sitting on his wife's lap, all the while expecting another scold-ing from her, Khaye Devoyre, because he had dared to suggest that there was a possibility of her Chanele leaving Molits.

But Khaye Devoyre's thoughts were elsewhere. She was busy serving the food and keeping an eye on the "little one", meaning Chanele, and mak-ing sure that, God forbid, she did not drop the baby; and so she had already forgotten the whole business. Admittedly, when Menasseh had told her the news earlier it had made her nervous, but now, at the table, the whole affair seemed a long way away. It was like a dream: while you were having the dream, or when you had just woken up, it all felt incredibly real but a few moments later, when you started doing other things, you just forgot about it.

Molits had not forgotten, though. Far from it. The whole *shtetl* had fallen prey to the tortuous dilemma.

"How was it possible? Their rabbi! The pride of Molits! The great scholar! The great saint! Who did they think they were, these strange Jews from a another city, to come and take him away!"

"Molits will not allow this to happen!" These were the first words uttered at all the meetings and discussions. Everybody blamed everyone else. Although it was the middle of the week, Jewish workers had put on their Sabbath clothes to come to the synagogue and listen, maybe throw in a word or two themselves. Even the women were concerned that the rabbi, may he have a long life, should stay in Molits.

Pious, wealthy Jewish women were so agitated that their diamond earrings trembled. They pinched the beads on their hats nervously and twisted the fringes of their silken headscarves. They huddled in their fur coats, as if to derive comfort from them, while they were listening to every word the men had to say.

After considerable discussion the Molits community agreed that they would approach the rabbi later that afternoon. They would offer their apologies and ask him to stay. This had been a bitter pill to swallow for the council members, because as far as they were concerned the rabbi was just a child, while they were the respected elders of Molits.

Reb Meyerl had not set foot in the synagogue the whole day. He had prayed alone. He had also fasted again and it was only now, close to evening, that he had eaten a little. He had just finished reciting his prayers, and was about to start studying, when the door of the courtroom opened. Three Jews came in, dressed in heavy fur coats with raised collars and swathed in scarves. Their heads were covered in the most enormous caps, to prevent their ears freezing in the bitter cold.

Reb Meyerl got up when he noticed the visitors. Walking towards them he stretched out his large, brown hands and bade them welcome. He told them to get rid of their coats, and he called for Menasseh to take their dripping clothes away. While he offered them a seat, he also asked Menasseh to bring in the samovar. By sheer force of habit, the assistant placed the samovar in the middle of the table.

The Jews were hugging hot glasses with their frozen hands. As they sipped the tea, they almost groaned with enjoyment: "Ahhh, what a pleasure! So lovely and warm!"

Reb Meyerl glanced sideways at the wall and he realised that in a few moments his destiny would be determined. Would he really become the rabbi of Pilsk? Pilsk was a city, compared to Molits. On the other hand, he didn't feel like exchanging his small *shtetl* and his dear Jews - those simple, pious, sincere Jews of his. But the clock kept on ticking. The heavy, yellow weights were swinging quietly back and forth. The hands, especially the big one, were moving. And so the time had come.

At that exact moment a group of the most respectable members of the Molits community arrived at the rabbi's house (that is, at the house of his father-in-law, Avrom Aaron). Most of them were still standing at the door, while some had already entered the hallway. They were a few steps away from the rabbinical courtroom, when they noticed the rabbi. He looked pale and taller even than usual, his eyes penetrating and serious. They saw how he got up from his chair, unaware of their presence, and they could see him glance at the clock and mumble to himself:

"They didn't come."

And turning around to the Jews from Pilsk he said something with a voice so soft and serious it almost sounded like a prayer.

"*Mazl tov*, rabbi of Pilsk!" the Jews from Pilsk were positively beaming.

Only now did Reb Meyerl notice the dignitaries from his own town. But it was too late. He could not take his words back anymore.

And all this because the Molits delegation had arrived five minutes too late, they had spent so long agonising. Feeling remorseful about the relief he had felt earlier, he knew he had to atone for his sin; but against his own will, there was a joyful tremor deep in his heart, even at that moment.

"Well, this is the way it was meant to be," his father-in-law called out.

"Apparently, Providence has decided in this way," Reb Meyerl replied softly, as he sat there lost in thought.

"Goodnight, rabbi," the group from Molits said quietly as they prepared to leave. But the head of the worthies from Pilsk was in such high spirits that he invited them to make a toast together. The locals, on the other hand, were keen to leave as quickly as possible. But then their leader, the fat one who was already standing at the door, paused a moment and walked back to the table. He offered the rabbi his hand, mumbled something that nobody understood and then quickly added out loud: "May you be successful, rabbi!" The others repeated the words after him and then they left the bright, warm courtroom, which had seemed so *heymish*, homely and comfortable.

Menasseh brought the vodka and they all made a toast. After that, the Jews from Pilsk immediately felt at home. They agreed that they would return to Pilsk that same week, together with their new rabbi. After they had made all the preparations and the rabbi's wife was ready, they would come and collect her as well.

"So, has it turned out the way you wanted or not?" Avrom Aaron asked his son-in-law, slightly worried.

"God forbid! The way Providence wanted." Reb Meyerl felt a gnawing sense of nostalgia, as if he had already been away for years - from his home, from the *shtetl* where he had grown up, married and become rabbi.

This feeling of nostalgia would stay with him for the rest of his life. Within a few years he became a person of great renown. The invitations to become rabbi elsewhere kept pouring in from the biggest cities, because by then he was no longer the rabbi from Molits, but the *Gaon* of Pilsk. But Reb Meyerl was simply not interested in going anywhere else. One sin was enough.

"It is absolutely extraordinary how much Reb Meyerl cares for Pilsk," people from elsewhere remarked. They could not understand the reason and they were envious of the city.

"Do you have a cemetery there?" he would ask when people became ever more persuasive.

"What kind of a question is that? Of course we have a cemetery," these respectable Jews answered with a big smile.

"We have one in Pilsk as well!" Reb Meyerl smiled back at them, and that was the end of it.

# *Shloyme*

If it was up to Shloyme he would not lift a finger from one end of the year to the next.

Even begging is too much for him. He would rather go hungry, dreaming away the day, nestling on other people's doorsteps, as free as the air. His skinny feet are covered in dried mud. They look as if they have been kneaded from clay. He has a small, pale face on which you can hardly see his little nose for the dirt around it.

The eleven-year-old causes a lot of trouble to the women in the *shtetl*. They know they will never be able to turn him into a "good" boy.

"Sholemke, if I catch you one more time on the steps next to my shop, I will tear you to pieces, that's what I'll do! Beat it! Get out of here! Do you hear me?" The shopkeepers chase him away like a dog. Shloyme never even looks at them but stays exactly where he is, pulling his coat over his red, frozen ears.

But when hunger starts to gnaw at him, he gets up, shakes off the dust and goes off in search of food.

"Can you give me a piece of bread? Can you give me a pie?"

"Be off with you! Go away! There is no bread here! You aren't ill! You can work! What kind of charity would it be to give you anything? To help raise a thief, hmmm! What will become of you?" Though they felt a little guilty, the women only offered a few crumbs of comfort. "What a shame to go around begging like an orphan. God forbid!"

"Can you give me a piece of bread? Can you leave me a few..."

"Get out, I said! Or otherwise I'll throw this bucketful of slops over your head!"

But Shloyme knows the routine already: he won't budge. When they try to give him stale bread, he refuses it. He only has to give them one look, one flash of those big, burning eyes that stare out at them from his dirty little face, and he can break their resolve. They don't understand why but they all give him something in the end: a baked roll, a piece of fresh bread, a cracker, depending on what's been baking on the day. Instead of thanking them, Shloyme gives them an impish smile, and off he goes.

"Go to hell, you big fat cows!" he shouts at them while his sharp little teeth break pieces off their tasty crackers.

"Sholemke, do you want to earn a few groschen, Sholemke?"

"I don't want to earn anything!"

"Sholemke, a *mitsve*, a good deed - and money with it!"

"I don't give a damn about *mitsves*!"

"And money, Shloyme, what about money?"

"I don't want anything!"

"To hell with you! Just try begging here again!" The women are seething with rage.

Shloyme does not answer. Instead, he whistles so loudly that he almost chases away the wintry clouds. Then he just skips away.

"It's a sin that such a creature is allowed to grow up in a Jewish community. It's a *khilul hashem*, a blasphemy against God," the wife of the synagogue warden says, proud to show off her Hebrew.

"Shloyme, I will turn you inside out and chop you up, if you don't stop giving us a bad name. You scum! Woe to your mother who brought you into this world!" Every Friday evening his father, Hershl the idiot, creates such a racket that their shabby little house shakes to its very foundations.

Shloyme's big eyes stare at his feet and he says nothing. He knows his father is right. He also knows that his father will get up, take off his belt and start roaring at him. He will stretch himself out so that it seems as if he is supporting the whole ceiling. He will shrug his shoulders and shake his broad, square beard. Eventually, he will put his belt back around his patched-up trousers, loosen his fists and throw himself back upon the straw mattress with such force that the bed creaks under his weight.

Afterwards he will call him, Shloyme, and ask him to take off his heavy boots and undo the bandages that are wrapped around his aching feet. The room will soon be filled by a powerful smell of sweat, and Shloyme will bring in a bowl of warm water of his own accord. His father will then soak his feet and groan with pleasure: "Ah-ah-ah-oy!"

Shloyme's sister, Shoshe, will arrive looking smart, wearing a clean pinafore dress, her hair done up like a landowner's wife. She will be wearing two golden earrings which she has received as an engagement gift from her fiancé. She will conjure up a piece of cooked chicken out of her pinafore, as well as two pieces of fish and a small, shining, plaited loaf of *challah* for the Sabbath.

Shloyme's mother will not want to accept it. Shoshe will swear by her betrothed that his mother knows about it. In the end, Shloyme's mother will take the food with a big sigh and Shloyme will be happy. His mother will spread out two torn towels on the small table instead of a cloth. She will then go back to the little black oven to finish preparing the watery potato soup. She will carefully put two tiny candles in the small, clay candlesticks, which he has made for her. It won't be long before she starts telling him off:

"Your father is a saint. You should be glad that he hasn't broken all your bones yet! How many times do we have to tell you not to go begging?"

She will show him her hands: "Look at these hands. Who do you think they are working for if not for you? Does your father have to come home on Friday, broken from a week's hard work, to be shamed on the Sabbath by that thief Khetskel in the synagogue? To be shown up in public! To be told in front of everyone that he should stop sending his son out to beg! You could work in Khetskel's butcher's shop, for heaven's sake. But no, begging is easier!

"So we are making you beg? And what about Shoshe? Aren't you putting her to shame as well? She is about to get married and I tremble when I imagine what could happen to her engagement because of you."

Shloyme thinks to himself. "Why don't you give me enough to eat then? And Shoshe the golden bride - she doesn't care for me one little bit. And Khetskel? May he rot in hell! He kicks me like a dog for no reason at all." His eyes burn like torches but he does not say a word. He looks at his mother with pity and clenches his small fists, thinking of Khetskel, of Shoshe, and of a way to escape.

"Your father won't go to the synagogue at all today; that's for sure."

Shloyme is startled out of his thoughts. It is only now that he hears the heavy snoring that fills the room.

"Oh, don't worry about it," says Shloyme.

"Come on, go and wash. It's Friday night, the start of the Sabbath. Take a look at yourself!"

"Tomorrow, mother, tomorrow I will wash myself in the lake. The water is already warm, just as warm as in the middle of summer."

"Tomorrow you will take a bath! On the Sabbath?" his mother exclaims in horror. Then she sighs.

Hershl moves around on his mattress. The small bed creaks. He rubs his eyes and looks at the room around him for a while like a total stranger.

"Have you already 'cursed' the Sabbath candles?" he jokes, and scratches his beard with satisfaction.

He gets out of bed, wraps a bag around his bare, swollen feet, takes a seat at the head of the table and starts to make the blessing over the wine to observe the start of the Sabbath. He forgets that he has not said either his afternoon or evening prayers.

The cheap fat is trickling down the clay candlesticks; the candles have nearly burnt out. The little flames are quivering. The shadows on the dirty walls are dancing madly.

"What else do we have? There is only one *challah* here."

Shloyme pulls a roll out of one of his pockets and places it next to the *challah*.

Hershl gets up and towers over him menacingly:

"May the earth swallow you up, you little thief!"

"Father, I swear by all that is holy that the synagogue caretaker gave that roll to me for polishing the menorahs. He couldn't do it himself because he was ill."

His father believes him.

He begins: "It was the sixth day; heaven and earth were finished." He pulls the bag tighter around his feet, cuts the small *challah* into pieces and hands them around. He does not touch the roll. Shloyme's mother gives his father a piece of the fish. She divides the other piece in two. She spoons out the boiling potato soup and adds small crumbs of chicken to it. She hardly takes any of it for herself. Shloyme is happily sucking his dirty fingers as well as the chicken bones.

That's how it is all year long, but not on the days leading up to Passover. Just before Passover, Shloyme will do anything. He is on his feet from morning to night. The women know this and they happily abuse it:

"Sholemke, will you come and help me make the dishes kosher?"

"Sure!"

"Sholemke, please carry this basket home for me, will you?"

"No problem!"

"Sholemke, you little *mamzer*, can you help me pluck the chickens this week?"

"Absolutely!"

He even gives Khetskel a hand.

He does not have to beg. The women give him bread, almond cakes, biscuits, pastries - all the things they have not allowed themselves for the whole year and kept aside for a special occasion. And now they have to get rid of all traces of leavened dough. They also give him old rags and leftovers of vegetables. Shloyme sells everything for cash. He is very pleased with himself.

Their little house is sparkling clean. It looks lovely now. A white, cotton bundle is hanging down from the low ceiling in the centre of the room, full of freshly baked matzos. Shloyme does not allow himself as much as a glance in their direction, for fear of making them dirty just by looking at them. But he does occasionally check the barrel in the corner in which big chunks of beetroot are left to pickle. When he sees everything is fine, he is satisfied and closes the lid.

He does not see his mother and father at all. He is much too busy to miss them.

And then the eve of Passover arrives. His parents have prepared everything. The clay candlesticks have been made festive with red crepe paper. A new cloth is lying on the table. Special foods are laid out for the Seder, the Passover service and meal remembering Jewish slavery and redemption in Egypt. The matzos almost take one's breath away with their freshness. There are at least six pieces of fish, decorated with carrot slices presented appetisingly on a long dish. The rich redness of the wine glistens inside a slightly chipped carafe. Small portions of *kharoset*, a sweet dish of chopped fruits and nuts ground up into a paste with wine, are arranged on plates. The hard-boiled eggs have been peeled. They are shining and there is a hint of blue around each yolk. Even the salt water looks appetising. Large candles are burning in the candlesticks today.

Shloyme looks at everything with rare respect. He does not dare to touch a thing. He is waiting for that special moment, the beginning of the Seder he loves so much that he would give up half his life for it. He is sitting there on his polished crate. His father looks like a king on his white cushion at the head of the table, his mother opposite him. The light of the polished candlesticks burnishes everybody with a golden glow. Shloyme is dressed in a new suit. His cheeks are glowing and his big eyes are burning. His heart is full of joy.

"Ah, *Pesach!*" he almost cries out loud in sheer delight. He is sure that he knows every word of the four questions by heart. And just at that moment his father nods at him and Shloyme begins:

"*Ma nishtane ha'layla ha'ze*? Why is this night different from all other nights...?"

# Jewish Nobility

Even though he had never mentioned it to anyone, everyone in the *shtetl* knew that Hershel was saving up so that one day he would be able to marry his daughter to a scholar.

Everybody knew that he regretted being a tailor, and that deep in his heart he resented the fact that his mother, who was no longer alive, had encouraged him to become a craftsman.

Hershel's father had been a scholar, a God-fearing man, and as poor as Job. Being someone who never had any luck, he had held out great hopes for his son.

"Hershel," he would say, "sit down and study. You are a clever boy. You just have to want it. And if you want it enough, with God's help, you will become a rabbi." But fate had decided otherwise.

Hershel's mother was descended from a family of simple, ignorant Jews. Immediately after her husband's death, she decided that Hershel had to be taught a trade, and she had taken him to a tailor. This had been particularly painful for Hershel as he was already studying at the yeshiva. He had even taught himself Russian to increase his chances at the rabbinical examination and to help him find a position afterwards. He never wanted to suffer as his unfortunate father had done.

When he was twenty years old, instead of warming a bench in the *yeshiva*, Hershel was slaving away at a sewing machine. Day in, day out, he tacked and sewed and pressed, and before he knew it, he had become the best tailor in Zhelechits.

"He may have a head for the Talmud," people in the *shtetl* said, "but his talents certainly don't end there!"

Hershel put on a brave face. Although it disturbed him to be an artisan, doing his job gave him satisfaction, as it allowed him to provide for his mother and the other children now that their father was dead. And if, at times, his heart was assailed by a deep longing for a rabbinical throne instead of his humble wooden workbench, he would comfort himself with the thought that Yonathan ha-Sandlar had been a craftsman too - a cobbler.

His daily outfit was not that of a tailor, but of a Hasid. On the Sabbath he always wore a silk gabardine and a small velvet hat. He prayed at the front of the synagogue, among the other Hasids of the *shtetl*; and he often went to the rabbi's home as an honoured guest for the closing meal of the day. He prepared himself to do that which his own father had done years ago, namely to make sure that the boys would grow up to be fine Jews, and that the girls would get fine husbands. For Hershel, "fine" meant having an aptitude for religious learning.

Hershel knew that his boys were good at learning and the rabbi would confirm this every time Hershel sent them to him to be tested.

"Reb Hershel, your children are good, thank God! They can and want to learn, thank God!"

These conversations with the rabbi always raised Hershel's spirits, and he would forget any resentment that he might otherwise feel. He then worked with renewed energy and great enjoyment, softly humming a Hasidic melody. At such moments, he was convinced that everything was meant to be this way. It was Providence that had made his mother force him to become a tailor. Just imagine: if he had been poor, God forbid, he would not have the money to pay a teacher for the boys. He would not be able to provide a dowry for his sisters, and they would be obliged, God forbid, to marry simple, uneducated Jews.

Thinking along these lines, his mood improved even more and he started singing out loud. His two journeymen joined in. A jubilant atmosphere soon filled the whole house. The shopkeepers, standing idly in their doorways, waiting for customers who did not come, heard the joyful sounds and they could not hide their jealousy.

"He's a lucky Jew, that Hershel," they sighed. Binyomen the tailor was his greatest enemy. The other people in the town called Binyomen "the wanderer" because he had to travel increasingly far afield to beat Hershel at finding customers among the farmers. Nobody ever heard him sing. He had no reason to. He barely scraped a living. All his children had left; the girls worked as servants in Warsaw and both his sons had joined the military. He had a cold and lonely heart. He blamed Hershel for taking away his source of income. It was all Hershel's fault, because he was so much better at his trade than he was, in spite of the fact that Binyomen was descended from a long line of tailors.

"It's the evil eye," Binyomen muttered to himself.

Even though Hershel worked very hard, he and his family lived frugally. They ate black bread with herring for breakfast and gruel for supper. On weekdays there was not even a slice of meat on their plates. On the Sabbath Khaye-Beyle, Hershel's wife, sometimes bought a cow's head or foot, and occasionally a piece of lung or liver, but only for her husband and for the boys. She, her daughters and the workers could no longer remember the taste of meat.

Hershel stood bent over the long workbench near the window for the whole day, and often part of the night as well. He was very careful at drawing the outlines of the patterns. The piece of chalk in his hand glided confidently over the material, whether it was the coarse cloth of a peasant garment or a piece of shiny silk, which would end up around the shoulders of a local landowner or a Hasidic Jew. Whoever they were, they were all anxious to have their clothes made by Hershel.

He would take a long time before actually cutting the fabric. When he finally sat down at the sewing machine, he worked with such fervour that his two assistants, who had been quietly stitching away until then - they had no reason to hurry - became infected by his enthusiasm. Hershel's machine rattled so excitedly that they unconsciously increased their speed, as if they too needed to save money for their future sons-in-law.

Opposite them, next to the other window, stood Sarah, Hershel's eldest daughter. Just like her father, she measured and drew patterns, the piece of chalk sliding over the silk and woollen fabric. She sewed for the "finest ladies" in the town. Among her clientele, there was the wife of a rich man, who did not patronise any of the other seamstresses in Zhelechits, but who had most of her clothes made in Warsaw.

One day the *shtetl* had a surprise visit. It had been a fine summer's day. Everyone had been basking in the sunlight. The air was saturated with the fragrance of acacia trees and the smell of the ripe fruit emanating from the nearby orchards. The birds had been singing cheerfully; a bit like Hershel himself on days when the rabbi praised his sons for their intelligence. That day the entire *shtetl* witnessed how the wife of a wealthy landowner had arrived at Hershel's house. Not even Warsaw was good enough for this woman; she normally had her wardrobe made in Paris. She had taken Sarah with her, in order to have her measurements taken in the privacy of her mansion, after which she had ordered a whole series of light, summer frocks that she would wear during her stay at a spa abroad.

Sarah was very slender, so people mockingly called her "Hershel's model". Sarah could not have cared less. She knew they said it out of jealousy. People held a grudge against her because she had such high-class customers, and because she and her father had managed to put aside so much money for her dowry, that one day she might marry a rabbi and become a *rebbetsin*. When she thought about this, her big black eyes would suddenly light up. They shone with pride and contentment and she too began to sing.

Sarah's moral conduct was as strict as that of her father. She did not make friends with any of the common girls in the *shtetl*. This meant she had no friends at all, since the daughters of the well-off Jews snubbed her for being a seamstress and the daughter of a tailor.

Her younger sister, Toybe, helped her with the needlework, and like Sarah, she often did not get any fresh air for days on end. However, unlike Sarah, her behaviour was not impeccable. She was only seventeen, but she was already involved in an illicit love affair with someone who was not exactly a rabbi either!

Her lover was an apprentice with his older brother, Leybish, the baker. Leybish had managed to get a contract to supply bread to the army base right next to Zhelechits. As if that was not good enough, he also ran his own food shop. He was indeed a rich man. If Leybish had not been an ignoramus, Hershel could have been quite pleased with such a match. After all, Nechemia, Toybe's beloved, did not need any dowry so it could have been perfect.

But Hershel was not looking for a match for Toybe. He was completely unaware of her burning desire to get married. He did not even know that his daughter was in love.

Toybe was tall and slim. She had a pair of glittering black eyes, just like her older sister, and long, dark hair. While she was at work, the curls danced merrily around her smiling face - how could Hershel have guessed that this had anything to do with love? She had always been a naughty child who could never sit still.

Another thing that had never occurred to Hershel, nor to Sarah for that matter, was to pay Toybe for her work.

"She's a real blessing, that girl, may no harm come to her," Hershel thought from time to time when he saw her working hard at her sewing machine, or when he noticed how expertly she added the finishing touches to a piece of work. All that fire she had within her seemed to flow into her needle and into the numerous songs that Nechemia had taught her.

Khaye-Beyle worked like a dog. All year she stood at the hot stove, rattling the enormous skillets in which she fried never-ending piles of onions. She could be seen running around the market to buy food, always on the lookout for bargains. Or else she busied herself with the laundry, in the courtyard during the summer and indoors in winter. She never took a rest, other than at the times when she had to sit down anyway to fold or repair clothes.

This was how things were during the week, but the Sabbath was different. On the Sabbath Hershel went to bed after lunch for a nice long nap. He fell asleep in no time, buried deep under a heavy eiderdown regardless of the season. Thus he killed two birds with one stone: he built up strength for a whole week, and he performed a commandment by observing the Sabbath as a day of rest.

Sarah would usually sit on a stool, which she had taken out on the street, and read a chapter of the *Tenakh* or other holy writings. Afterwards she too would relax on the sofa bed in the alcove where Toybe and she both slept, and read innocent romantic novels.

The boys spent the afternoon with the teacher.

For Khaye-Beyle Saturday afternoon was the time to have a chat with her neighbours. She felt at ease among these simple women, who were her friends. They would all sit down together on the threshold of Gedalya's grocery store. Khaye-Beyle would tell them how hard it was for her to make ends meet and how she did not even come near a piece of lung or liver the whole week long.

"Not that I'm asking for a piece of meat during the week, God forbid. May I not be punished for saying this, but really, I'm sick and tired of food that tastes like gruel. I feel sick if I just smell it!"

The women would wink at each other and say to her that she only had herself to blame. If she was clever, she would know how to speak to Hershel and get him to open his wallet. There would be enough for her to have not only meat but even *tsimes*, stews of vegetables or fruits, during the week.

It hurt when they talked to her like this, but she liked their company too much to go home. She was incapable of taking a nap like her husband, or dutifully reading a book like her eldest daughter. So she pretended not to hear their spiteful remarks, for she enjoyed catching up on the latest gossip and picking up all the news she had missed because she had been too busy during the week.

Toybe's Saturday afternoons were not spent in studying Torah or with the neighbours. Nechemia would be waiting for her in the nearby forest, in Leybish the baker's orchard or simply in the open fields.

Nechemia was tall, even taller than Toybe and just as slender. He had blond hair and clever, blue eyes. Despite their light colour his eyes had such a penetrating expression that Toybe felt scorched by his mere gaze. Recently he had begun to kiss her as well. Toybe knew they shouldn't do this and that it was a terrible sin, but what could she do when his burning lips almost suffocated her? And why deny it? She too was possessed by a feverish desire. She did not really want him "to stop it", as she kept pleading with him while pressing her body even closer to his.

Both of them were healthy and young, and very much in love with one another. If it had been up to them, they would have married then and there - on the Sabbath.

In the meantime, Hershel was sound asleep. He was busy building up his strength for the week ahead, and doing what every good Jew was supposed to be doing on the Sabbath: rest. Even in his wildest dreams he could not have known about this; his youngest daughter lying with Nechemia in a field, where no Jew would normally go. None of the other boys and girls, who slipped away in secret after lunch, ever strayed that far. It was very close to the next village, where only non-Jews lived. Toybe and Nechemia would lie in the field, or else in a remote corner of the forest, under a fragrant pine tree, or in Leybish the baker's orchard. They lay there in each other's arms, kissing one another, like *goyim*.

Nechemia's father was a butcher. He was a tall man with a broad, bony face. He had a thatch of blond hair, which was going grey, on top of which was perched a small cloth hat. His long hair hung down from underneath the hat on both sides of his face and merged with his beard, covering most of his neck. Day in, day out, he wore a pair of boots covered in blood and mud, the legs of his trousers tucked deep inside them, and a shiny apron, which had bloodstains on it.

Nechemia's mother was the exact opposite. She was small and thin, and her dresses were invariably spotless and neatly ironed. On her head she wore a cap, adorned with little ribbons. It stood precisely in the middle of her head, so that one could see her thick, red hair peeping out from all sides. Unlike all the other women in the *shtetl*, she was not in the habit of shaving it off.

She liked to sit on the threshold of her son Leybish's shop to observe how the business prospered, may no harm come to it. But often she was chased away by her daughter-in-law, who scolded her for being in the customers' way. Then she would remove herself and sit down in the street, on a small wooden stool, which she had filched from the bakery, unbeknownst to her daughter-in-law.

As she was sitting near her son's shop, she was never short of women to chat with. Word went round in Zhelechits, that it was because of her, Pinchas' wife, that the shop sold so much. There was nobody else in the *shtetl* with whom one could have such a pleasant chat, as with her. Most of the time her daughter was there too, a girl almost as tall as her father and with the same fiery red hair as her mother. She loved to talk with the other women as much as or even more than her mother did. In fact, she already looked like those women, even though she was not yet married.

Leybish and Nechemia were ashamed of their mother as well as their sister. Leybish had adopted a way of life which was suitable for a wealthy man. He gave generously to charity. One Sabbath, when he had been honoured with a Torah reading, he gave a large donation to the synagogue, for the poor. After that, he was treated as one of the most respected members of the community and he did not hold back his money. He gave with a sense of gratitude for his own prosperity. Although he was not in the least bit learned, the people in the little town did not regard him as a simple Jew. Moreover, his wife was refined. Her father had been the owner of a small kvass factory, and he had known a thing or two about the Talmud as well. What was more, his wife had black hair, which greatly impressed Leybish who was descended from a family of redheads. Nevertheless, even though it irritated him, he never reproached his mother with the fact that she sat on his doorstep the whole day long.

Leybish also felt he had nothing to be ashamed of as far as Nechemia was concerned. The boy was following in his footsteps. It also pleased Leybish that Nechemia had chosen a girl who would make an honourable addition to the family.

But then, suddenly, everything changed.

Pinchas' wife no longer sat in the doorway of her son's store. Misfortune had struck the family of Pinchas the butcher. It was his middle son, Mendel.

In the past, more than one mother with grown-up daughters had wished to have him as a son-in-law: "What a treasure, that boy is," they would say.

"He's a real fixer! Who do you think arranged that contract for Pinchas to deliver meat to the military? Of course, it was him! It's because of Mendele that his father's business does so well. He is another Leybish in the making."

He had been the star of the family. His mother doted on him, more than on any of her other children: "There is no one like my Mendele." She never stopped singing his praises to the other women in the community. He was a great help to his father, tirelessly combing the villages as he tried to find the best oxen and bulls for the army. He always managed to haggle and get the price down as well. All his father had to do was slaughter the animals, and Mendel often gave him a hand there too. He did most of the delivery work as well.

"Father," he would say, "you just stay here on the wagon to make sure that nobody steals anything, and I'll take care of the rest! You only have to sit here like an emperor on your throne and guard the meat. Are you listening to me, father? Mendele will do the rest. Trust me. I'm better at this than those crooks. Ha! Ha! Ha!"

The last thing this golden boy needed was for a *shikse*, a non-Jewish girl, to fall in love with him. However, that is exactly what happened. It was more than falling in love. She became obsessed with him. She followed him around everywhere and used all the tricks she had in her power to charm him. It did not take her long to convince him that he was in love with her as well. And because of this *shikse* with her round, pockmarked face, he had left the *shtetl* and converted. He had ruined the life of his parents and brought misery upon his brothers.

The "house" of Pinchas the butcher sank into despair. Pinchas himself turned grey overnight. He stopped eating. He could hardly speak. He turned into a mere shadow of his former self. As soon as the seven days of mourning for Mendel were over, he closed his shop. From then on he just wandered around the *shtetl* with his long, unkempt hair and beard. He no longer combed them, and he did not allow anyone else to touch them either. He had an air of melancholy and the little boys in the *shtetl* started calling him "crazy Pinchas". He never uttered a single word to anyone, so people began to avoid him.

Pinchas' wife had become smaller, even more shrivelled than before. There was nothing left of her.

Her red hair turned completely grey. Her little cap was dirty all the time. Her dress stuck to her body. She sat alone at home the whole day and never stopped crying. Mendel's sister had gone to live with a relative in Warsaw. She never came home any more. The sight of her parents' disgrace was too much for her. The house was no longer a house but a grave, she said. And she was right.

Leybish did not show his distress though his heart was full of bitterness. Nechemia said that his brother deserved to be killed.

What Nechemia didn't know of course, was that his brother was close to killing himself. Mendel racked his brain day and night, about how he could get out of this new milieu he found himself in. Already on the day of his marriage, when he was about to enter the church, the whole thing suddenly seemed hateful to him. As soon as he heard the unintelligible chanting and smelled the incense, as soon as he saw the priest in his white robes, an awful memory came back to him from his childhood. He could not help thinking about all the Maundy Thursdays when the Jews of his *shtetl* had been terrorised with fear. This was the same priest who used to walk slowly around their marketplace, dressed in the same white robes with the same large cross on his chest, accompanied by white-clad girls, who carried around a statue of a baby and his mother in their arms while chanting just as they did now for his wedding. He also remembered how once, during the High Holidays, he and some other children had been left at a neighbour's house, while their parents were in the synagogue. Suddenly he had heard people screaming outside. He left the house to see what was happening and saw the streets filled with peasants. They were wielding hatchets and iron bars. Just at that moment their parents had come running in, their faces twisted with fear. They had quickly grabbed their children, locked all the doors and windows, and sat down in complete silence. That night the *shtetl* burned.

He had been very young at the time. He had forgotten all about it until the moment he stood in front of the altar with his bride, when those awful images came back with great intensity. He felt a sudden urge to spit in the faces of those around him. He wanted to run back to his mother and father, and never in his life be a non-Jew again. But it was too late. A sense of fear took hold of him, just like when he was a little boy. He saw them right in front of him, hatchets and bars in their hands. He heard wild screams all around him. Everything had become just like that day long ago. For a moment he thought the church was on fire.

Although his father-in-law was not a poor man, who even owned a bit of land, the family lived simply, like wretched peasants.

Mendel, who by now was called Matchek, had to eat from the same bowl as his wife's younger brother and sister, as well as her drunken father. His breath stank of alcohol and tobacco all the time, and "Matchek" was disgusted by the way everybody dug into the same bowl. It made him gnash his teeth in anger. The food stuck in his throat. He also could not stand the smell of pork, which filled the whole cottage when his wife was frying onions. He knew that she always cut bits off the large brown piece of smoked pork meat, which hung constantly on a hook next to the oven. There were worms creeping out of it, long white worms.

Whenever they had a fight - which happened quite often - she would yell at him, "You filthy Jew!"

His own family did not know anything about all this. They had erased him from their memory and never mentioned his name.

Old Pinchas no longer thought about anything these days. His mind had gone completely blank. But his tiny wife, who had also aged enormously, had not forgotten her son entirely. Every time she remembered how they had torn their clothes as a sign of mourning for their "dead" son, she started crying all over again. The fact that she still loved him, made her feel guilty, as if her feelings were sinful. She never stopped having dreams about him, mostly sad ones, but once in a while a happy one too.

Sometimes he appeared in her dreams as a small child still, sometimes as a tall, handsome young man towering over her. She even dreamt about him coming back home, throwing himself in her arms and weeping: "Oh mother, I don't want to go back to those *goyim*, mother don't make me go back! Mother!"

On such nights she would call out loud in her sleep: "Don't go away, Mendele, don't go! Stay here! Stay! Stay!" Or else she would scream: "Why are you mourning for him? He is alive!" Waking up confused and with a heavy heart, she would ask whether he had left again. Then she remembered everything and realised it had only been a dream. Tears streamed down her face.

It happened in the middle of the day as well. She would suddenly remember that awful mourning scene and she muttered to herself: "I wish they had killed me too, my child." Her own words terrified her.

In the meantime, Toybe and Nechemia grew more and more impatient. Even though they enjoyed their Sabbaths together, it was no longer enough for them. They longed for each other and wanted to be together all the time. They felt it was time to get married.

All the things they could not get enough of in the past - the long, romantic walks among the fragrant pine trees, the twittering of the birds, the hunts for fallen pine cones, the playful wrestling in the grass and the mouthfuls of juicy black cherries from Leybish's orchard - seemed less than exciting to them now. However, they did not have the slightest idea how to make their wish come true.

They knew very well that Hershel would never agree to this match.

For a long time they racked their brains. It caused them sleepless nights. They thought long and hard, and all they came up with was to get married secretly without Hershel's knowledge.

In Hershel's home, they had been obliged to tighten their belts even further recently, now that it had been decided that Sarah was going to get married. Her future husband was a diligent student, a descendent of a long line of scholars.

It was early morning. The *shtetl* was still covered by a light film of dew. Thin trails of mist slowly glided through the streets. The sun was about to break through and it would not be long until the glistening drops had evaporated. The little, leaning cottages huddled close together in their sleep. At this hour of the day, they seemed even smaller than usual. Somewhere shutters were opened. There was a rattling sound of an iron grille being removed from a shop window. Jews were already coming back from the first prayers in the synagogue, with their prayer shawls and phylacteries, under one arm, when one could hear muffled noises coming from the narrow river, which ran just behind the *shtetl*. A couple of small, black boats were tied up to the shore. They had come from Zakrotchin. A few women, future in-laws of Sarah, climbed out of the boats, eager to inspect the bride.

They had left the future bridegroom behind in the yeshiva where he studied. His mother, a Cossack of a woman, ran a small, struggling shop with leather goods in Zakrotchin. She was quick to whisper a secret into every-body's ear, while urging them not to pass it on, especially not to Hershel. The secret concerned her noble background.

"Oh," she complained, "it is so painful. If only my husband, may his memory be blessed, were still alive, we would have never given our consent to a match with a tailor. Hershel knows this. He knew my husband very well. Everybody knew my husband. But what can I say? I am just a poor widow."

The women of the *shtetl* listened patiently to this conceited relative whose tiny head was adorned with a gigantic satin hat. They noticed how her double chin quivered nervously, how she kept fingering the decorations on her hat, and they were all "deeply sympathetic" to her suffering.

After Hershel had agreed to provide the couple with full board and lodging, in what had been the alcove where the girls slept, and a considerable dowry on top of that, the woman decided that Sarah was a very nice girl indeed, and that settled the matter.

Hershel was delighted. Such a pedigree and such a fine person; it was more than he had hoped for. Hershel knew the young man from the time when he himself had studied at the yeshiva in Radzimin. "Yes, I worked so hard for it, and now I've got what I wanted, blessed be His name. It has all been worth it. Praise to the Lord above!" Hershel almost spoke the words out loud.

The marriage was to take place in six weeks' time. Hershel was keen to get hold of the bridegroom as soon as possible. The boy's mother agreed, even though she made it clear to Hershel that she was not in any great hurry. Though deep inside she knew very well that she could not have supported her son for very much longer.

In Hershel's home everybody worked incessantly on the preparations for the wedding. Hershel sewed from early in the morning till late at night, whether for the bridegroom or himself, the little boys, or for the Jews of the *shtetl* who all seemed to have waited for this one occasion to order a new silk gabardine.

Sarah was simply drowning in work. She was responsible for her own outfit in addition to all the clothes she had to make for her mother, her sisters and all the women of the *shtetl*.

Toybe laboured hard and suffered deep inside. She became paler every day. She would shed tears on the wedding dress, leaving marks on the precious fabric.

The bridegroom came down on a Sabbath. He was tall and pale, with black, curly hair and side curls, and a pair of dark blue eyes. He had girlishly red lips and small, white hands. His beard was black and short.

Sarah fell in love with him immediately.

The whole house revolved around Sarah. Nobody even looked at Toybe anymore. Recently Sarah had started treating her differently, as if she felt superior to her younger sister.

Toybe began to hate her sister and her father. Despite all her efforts to help Sarah with the preparations for the wedding, she had never received a word of gratitude. On the contrary, Sarah ordered her around as if she was some kind of apprentice girl.

Toybe suffered in silence. Only on the Sabbath did she pour her heart out to Nechemia. Then she expressed all the bitterness which she had bottled up during the week.

Nechemia, who had never liked all that Hasidic mystical nonsense in the first place, now developed an even greater hatred for Hershel than he had felt for his converted brother.

It was the end of summer. For weeks on end the *shtetl* was held captive by the warm sunlight. The sun shone so fiercely, you had to hold a hand above your eyes in order to see the little houses, which were shimmering in the heat. There was not a single white cloud in the sky, which looked like a magnificent blue canvas stretched out high above the *shtetl*.

The pine trees in the nearby woods spread the pungent fragrance of the warm resin. Some cornfields had already been cut, others still lay there, brown and ripe. Here and there one could see neatly tied-up sheaves, ready to be taken into the barns. Because of the heat everything had become ripe much earlier than usual that year. The low fruit trees were almost bending down under their heavy load. Even winter fruits were ready to be picked.

On one of those days, many of Sarah's relatives descended on the *shtetl*. Her future mother-in-law had kept a close watch on the guest list. Only people of a certain status had been invited.

They had all arranged to stay with family or friends in the *shtetl*. Since Zhelechits was only a short distance from Zakrotchin people generally knew each other well. All the furniture and sewing equipment had been taken out of Hershel's home. The journeymen were sent home, so they would not be in the way.

The largest room was now full of long tables and benches, which the family had borrowed from the synagogue and neighbours. Some were newly made for the occasion by Moshe the carpenter.

New white cloths covered the tables, resplendent with all kinds of delicacies: cakes and spirits, various strudels and honey biscuits. There were long rows of plates with chopped fish. At the head of the table stood a large dish with two carp's heads, one for the bridegroom and one for the rabbi. A delicious smell wafted from a freshly baked, gigantic *challah*. In the alcove, the bridal bed was waiting, made up with new, dazzlingly white linen.

Gedalya, the grocer in whose house Hershel lived, had offered his largest room for the women and girls to dance in, and a smaller one for them to get changed in. The latter also served as an extra guest-bedroom for some of the women.

Hershel had invited the most respectable members of the community, and they had all come. Hershel would have nothing to do with the craftsmen and other ordinary folk that day.

It was almost evening. The bride and groom were on their way back from the synagogue courtyard where the marriage ceremony had taken place. A sea of coloured lights welcomed the newly wed couple back home.

Nearly all the men were dressed in silk gabardines, with fur-edged hats or little velvet ones on their heads. The young women wore skilfully styled wigs and dresses made of satin and velvet. Young girls and children even joined in the dancing of *Aheym fun der khupe*, "Coming home from the wedding". Blue, white and red ribbons bounced around the room. There were smiling faces everywhere. The green and violet sequins on the women's dresses and jackets glittered as they whirled around the room. The silk on the men's shoulders gave off a veritable sheen.

Sarah's eyes were filled with tears of happiness. She looked tiny, almost like a twelve-year-old girl, in her white outfit. Her thick, black hair, which would be shaved off the next day, seemed even darker from behind her white veil. Her little brown hand now had two rings on it: a diamond ring - which Hershel had given her when the engagement contract had been signed, while pretending that it was a present from the groom's mother - and a gleaming, gold wedding ring. She could not stop looking at it. She was overjoyed.

Hershel's little boys, Haim and Yosele, were dressed in brand-new silk gabardines and little satin hats. Their faces were red with excitement. They did not move from the bridegroom's side for a single moment.

The family of Leybish the baker also celebrated a wedding today. The best room in the house had been prepared, the flowery curtains washed and ironed.

Leybish's wife loved the sight of fresh flowers. For this special occasion, she filled the room with vases. As if to apologise for decorating the room in such a non-Jewish fashion, she had unearthed a wall-hanging she had embroidered years ago, before she was married, and hung it in a prominent position, where it would be clearly visible to the bride and groom, the rabbi and the other guests.

The tapestry depicted various scenes: the Jews on their way out of Egypt, angels ascending and descending Jacob's ladder, Joseph in Pharaoh's palace explaining the dream with the seven fat and the seven lean cows, and in the middle of all of this a flock of white sheep could be seen grazing in a green field. The embroidery covered half a wall and it told whoever looked at it that Leybish's wife was a good Jewish woman, despite the fact that she loved flowers.

The long table in the centre of the room was full of fine wines and liqueurs, cake and spirits, and all kinds of exquisite fruits from Leybish's own orchard.

The floorboards were so white it seemed as if they had been sanded, rather than just scrubbed.

The wine in the glass carafes sparkled in the bright light of the paraffin lamp, which brought out the silver gleam of the knives and forks on the table. Cups and glasses, normally kept aside for Passover, had been made kosher; they were now acceptable for a meal which contained bread.

Leybish and Nechemia were both dressed in long black coats with a white flower in the left lapel. Leybish had learned about this fashion as a guest at a wedding in the "German synagogue" in Warsaw, in the days that he worked there as a baker's apprentice.

Dressed identically, the two brothers resembled each other so closely that it was hard to tell which one of them was the bridegroom, except for the fact that Leybish had a short, yellow beard, while Nechemia, who was several years younger, was clean-shaven.

The rabbi was seated at the head of the table. He was one of those modern rabbis. Leybish had brought him in from Warsaw, where he was struggling hard to provide an income for his wife and a horde of little children. May no harm come to them. Unlike other rabbis, this one spent most of his time performing secret marriages and divorce settlements. If, at times, the demand was low for his presence at such ceremonies, he resorted to sewing aprons. This was a craft he had mastered during his time in America, from where he had returned after an economic crisis there.

The rabbi had a broad, fiery red beard and a pair of thick, fleshy lips.

He possessed a mouth full of strong, white teeth and his face was round and plump. His eyes were the most amazing amber colour. He was not a lucky man. Whenever he tried something new, it soon turned into a disaster. In the end he understood he was never going to be more than a simple rabbi on a poor street in Warsaw.

Now he sat there at the head of the table, waiting impatiently for the bride. On the very evening of Sarah's wedding, when she was dressed up anyway, Toybe had to slip away from among the women and the girls in Hershel's house, and go to another celebration, that of her own wedding.

For the first time in his life, Nechemia had been biting his nails. He paced up and down the decorated room, asking himself for the thousandth time: "Will she come, or will she lose courage at the last moment?"

Toybe arrived with a workaday coat flung over her wedding dress. As soon as she came in, there was a burst of applause. The family showered Toybe with kisses. Men and women kissed each other as well. Toybe was beside herself with joy.

Before she knew what was going on, they had erected the *chuppah*, the wedding canopy. The required *minyan* of ten men, for the service, seemed to have appeared out of nowhere. And there was Nechemia already, repeating a formula which the rabbi said out loud while Nechemia put the ring around her finger. A golden ring just like the one Sarah had. Kisses were exchanged again. Then it was time to enjoy the wedding meal.

Of course, Leybish would have liked to have invited more distinguished guests, especially on this occasion, when his son was marrying into such a noble family. Just imagine, a match with Reb Hershel! But it so happened that they had been obliged to organise the whole affair in secret. Even his guests had only been informed at the last moment about the true reason for the celebration. All he had said to them beforehand was that they would not regret it. None of these men had known that apart from himself, nine other Jews had also been invited.

The whole ceremony had taken place so fast, that even now, after the *chuppah* ceremony, these guests could hardly believe what had happened. But when Leybish invited them to sit down at the table, like close relatives, they were quick to do so. They tucked into the various dishes. The meal was delicious; the men had never tasted anything like it. One plate after another disappeared down their throats, washed down with generous helpings of wine. Leybish already felt sorry that he had put his best fare on the table for them.

"We should have just sent them home with a few extra guilders, these beggars," Leybish said to his wife, who had never liked the idea in the first place. She had not opposed it, however, since she did not want to upset her husband. She had also felt humiliated by the whole conversion story of her brother-in-law, and she hoped that bringing Toybe, a daughter of Hershel, into their family, would restore some of their lost honour.

Old Pinchas sat at the head of the table, next to the newlywed couple and the rabbi. As usual, he did not utter a single word. He did not touch the food or the drink either. Despite his new suit, which Leybish had ordered for him for the wedding, he looked just as wretched as always, with his hair and beard unkempt.

The groom's mother was in no better state. By now she had shrunk so much that she hardly reached the table. Just like her husband she looked miserable in her new outfit. What was left of her hair had turned completely white. It was just visible from underneath the delicate silken kerchief, which Nechemia had bought for her on the occasion of his wedding.

Toybe sat next to her husband, quiet and pale. Although the room was hot, she kept on shivering. The rabbi tried to cheer her up with anecdotes from the secret marriages he performed in Warsaw: "You should see how happy they are, these brides, they are beside themselves with joy!"

Toybe was crying.

Nechemia held her hand in his, trying to warm it with the heat of his own hand. He implored her to calm down, not to look so frightened. He kept filling up her glass, most of which he drank himself. Her lips barely touched the glass.

Suddenly she started crying even louder. She sounded just like a small child.

Velvel Shtok, the pedlar, stood up to his full height, and he gave such a hard bang on the table that it shook everything on it. He was dead drunk. He called out:

"No wonder the bride is crying! Just imagine, her father did not want to come to the wedding, the wedding of his own daughter. And why? Because the family isn't good enough for him. To hell with that bastard! Hasidic Jews are invited by him, but not us - ordinary, simple Jews. He is ashamed of us, that little tailor!" In his drunken outburst, Velvel poured out all the bitterness he had always felt towards the Hasidic Jews of the *shtetl*.

"Ah, what a great fellow you are! You are much better than all of us put together! Let's drink another toast to you, Leybish!" he cried out. He wanted to put his arm around Leybish, but he missed and landed on a bottle of wine. Amazed he stared at his fingers, which were full of blood and broken glass.

His speech had caused a stir. Leybish fled to the kitchen to find his wife and told her it was time to put an end to the meal.

"If we don't stop them now, we will never be able to get rid of them," he hissed.

The guests had no intention of leaving, though. There was no end to the drinking and cursing. They all got drunker and drunker.

"And you, Leybish, are you better than those Hasidic idiots? Would you have asked us to your daughter's wedding?" they stammered. By now they were just talking nonsense.

Some of them fell asleep at the table. These poor, wretched creatures were not used to good food and drink, and it knocked them out. They sat there, heads hanging down, and snored. Some of them still smacked their lips in their sleep, others talked out loud.

At that moment, Binyomen the tailor walked in. He had come to Toybe's wedding of his own accord. Nobody knew how he had found out about it. Leybish received him like a guest. He honoured him with a toast and invited him to the table.

But Binyomen did not want to take a seat. He had a drink, congratulated the newlywed couple and the relatives, and with a telling smile on his wrinkled face, left and went straight to Sarah's wedding.

The lights in the silver candlesticks had almost burned up by now. The rabbi was still talking about the speech the groom had given earlier. He praised him to the skies. "Reb Hershel, your son-in-law is a learned man, blessed be His name," the rabbi finally concluded.

The guests stood up. They were slightly tipsy from all the toasts and they were ready now for a bit of dancing. The women from the groom's side wiped their eyes, nearly choking with emotion. The groom's mother could barely restrain herself; she almost cried out loud from sheer exultation.

Khaye-Beyle watched them without saying a word. Deep down she could not stand the groom's mother and her Hasidic tricks.

Suddenly the door opened and Binyomen the tailor entered, looking gloomy and angry as always.

When Hershel noticed him, his heart skipped a beat. "He must be up to something," he thought, but what? Hershel stood up and walked over to him. When he stood very close to Binyomen, he asked him why he had come. Immediately, he felt sorry for what he had said. Today he wanted to be kind to everyone, even to his enemies, since God had granted him every reason to be proud and grateful.

"What I mean is, I'm happy to see you," he quickly added. "Let me pour you a glass of wine and together we will drink to my daughter's wedding."

"No need to bother," Binyomen answered with a smile. "I have already drunk a toast to the wedding of your younger daughter today. I should be so lucky! What a handsome couple they are, Pinchas the butcher's son and your daughter! As if God had ordained it. Apparently, you didn't want to come to Toybe's wedding. The family of Pinchas the butcher is not good enough for you it seems. So I went. It would be a sin to put a Jewish daughter to shame, wouldn't it, Reb Hershel? Now I'm here to wish you *mazl tov*. You have a lot of *mazl*, good fortune indeed, Reb Hershel, may no harm come to you. You have saved all that money to get one son-in-law, and now you've got two!"

Hershel looked at him bemused. He thought that Binyomen had lost his mind. What was he talking about? Toybe, a wedding? He was sure that he had seen Toybe dancing with the girls only a moment ago. He had seen it with his own eyes. The man had obviously gone completely mad.

"*Mazl tov! Mazl tov!* Congratulations! Congratulations! Dance Hasidim, dance!" Binyomen shrieked at the Jews in their silk gabardines and their fur-trimmed hats. They had formed a circle in the meantime and they were about to start a Hasidic dance.

"Dance! Reb Hershel deserves a double *Mazl tov*. He has become the relative of Pinchas the butcher. Reb Hershel has become twice as noble today!"

# The London Stories

# *Jim*

Jim gradually emerged through the fog. With long, thin, work-worn hands stretched out in front of him he felt his way carefully down a porter's alley, before arriving at the main street.

There, among the long line of lorries, cars and trams, which passed by on the wet asphalt, his tiny lamp started flickering as if it would give up the ghost at any moment. His face, which was almost as dark as the damp, black tarpaulin that protected the merchandise on his cart, had a pallid look and a sickly red glow around the pronounced cheekbones and hollow cheeks. The tip of his sharp, thin nose looked strangely pale. His half-open mouth revealed a couple of crooked, yellow teeth. Sharp, black bristles covered his chin. He spat into a dirty rag and was reassured when he saw there was no blood. He continued to dream about having a home of his own. It was his dearest wish. It kept him going, and gave him the strength he needed to do his job.

He was indeed a lucky Jim! Every week he took home thirty-five shillings. His income was not dependent on the seasons, like that of so many other workers in London. His boss was pleased with him. It sometimes happened that when he had worked particularly hard, his boss would show his appreciation by giving him a hearty slap on his narrow shoulders. Then Jim would grin and reveal a row of yellow teeth, by way of a smile. It made him feel so good, this friendly slap, that he failed to notice the hollow sound it made. Nor did he notice that he felt no pain. His eyes would simply get moist and shine like those of a grateful dog. He was happy because he had work and he no longer had to go all around London looking for factory work as he had done in the past.

He would never forget those times, like when his mother gave him sixpence with a trembling hand, telling him he had to eat, even though she knew all too well that he had to pay for so many other things with the money.

"If your father, blessed be his memory, were still alive, things wouldn't look so bleak," his mother had said, wiping away a tear.

"*I am lucky!*" Jim exclaimed and stopped his daydreaming. He was so excited he could not stop coughing. His cough sounded dry. He clasped his chest with one hand and held the other in front of his mouth. What a relief, no blood clots, not even a single drop!

A gleaming black Daimler indicated it had to park. Jim immediately moved his cart closer to the pavement. The car rolled softly into the parking space with an air of absolute disdain. It was as if it expected the whole of London to doff its hat.

The chauffeur got out of the car. He was wearing a brown uniform with shining, golden buttons and a pair of fur-trimmed leather gloves. He softly hummed a song, "*My darling, it isn't right, to sit alone in the park on a moonlit night*", as he walked into a shop.

Jim stood beside the gutter with his cart, crammed with boxes, and decided to have a rest.

"*He's a lucky fellow,*" Jim said to himself. He was jealous of the chauffeur. But he did not think much of the lady in the grey fur coat in the car. She looked like a dry old stick.

The chauffeur's gloved hands turned the steering wheel, and the car slid away with a self-satisfied purr, leaving behind the acrid smell of petrol and a mother-of-pearl shine on the wet road.

Jim smoked a cigarette. The lady in the car was still on his mind. He compared her to his girl in the box factory, and smiled to himself - what a difference! He looked at the cart and checked that the tarpaulin was still in place. He tightened the rope and harnessed himself to the cart. Navigating the traffic with care, he gradually got into the middle lane again.

He turned off at the street by the shoe factory where he had to make a delivery of a load of boxes. He pulled the bell next to the entrance. A small boy with short hair came running down and opened the door.

Brushing aside a lock of hair, he rubbed his face and greeted Jim like an old friend: "*Hello* Jim, you could have whistled! What did you ring the bell for, you idiot!"

"*Go away, shrimp.*" He was irritated by the boy's cheek and thought how nice it would be to be able to whistle. He twisted his mouth in a comical way, and it was hard to tell at that moment if he was laughing or crying.

The boy wanted to carry the boxes upstairs, but Jim would not let him.

"*Go away, you dog.*" That was the last thing he needed. The little imp might damage the boxes or make them dirty.

The cart was empty. Jim threw the tarpaulin and the rope inside. He smoked a cigarette which somebody had given him. Then he harnessed himself in again. He was happy that the job was done.

In the box factory, the girl who always made tea was already making her rounds, even though the bell had not yet rung. She crept silently, like a cat, between the piles of paper and the boards, trying not to trip over the wires, which were everywhere. Now and then, she looked furtively in the direction of the supervisor, who pretended not to notice her. She drank the tea, for which everybody, except for her, had to pay thruppence a week.

When Jim came upstairs, the long tables looked deserted; half-finished boxes were strewn all over the place, a pair of scissors were still stuck to a sheet of paper, a brush was left in a pot of glue. It seemed as if everything had been turned to stone by a magician's touch and the people round the tables had simply vanished.

In the break, the girls had a bite to eat, drank a *cup of tea*, and laughed at each other's stories. Some went out to powder their noses or put on some lipstick. The tea girl put all her make-up on again. She even took the trouble to brush her thin, mouse-coloured hair.

Jim looked around. All the crates were occupied, so he sat down on the steps leading into the office. He wiped the sweat from his brow and tried to get rid of some of the mud. He was waiting for his girl to bring him tea. He was so thirsty that his throat was itching.

"Hello, Jim!"

Jim looked up at the green metal lampshade on which a big fly was buzzing around, playing in the dust.

"Hello!"

She stood in front of him smiling, her face and lips made up in garish colours. Her cropped hair looked as if it had just been brushed. Her dress was short. It was well above her knees. She was holding a steaming cup of tea.

Jim thought about the lady in the Daimler and blushed. He shivered for a moment, afraid that she might guess his thoughts. He decided that his girl was very pretty indeed and that he would marry her one day. He would not listen to the doctor's advice. How could living alone and depressed, like a dog, be healthier than having a mate and a home. He thought about his savings, and he smiled with satisfaction. He had set aside every penny for this. Then he remembered that she was waiting with the tea. He hastily took the cup from her and almost scalded himself. The girl burst out laughing. She touched his moist, curly hair affectionately. As soon as she had sat down next to him on the steps, she started to tell him off: "Jim, just take a look at yourself! All the girls see you looking like this!"

Jim was ashamed of himself. He felt as if a needle was stuck between his ribs, sharp and pointed. It was such an odd sensation. When he talked to her, he always had the same feeling. She was so loyal. She always made sure he got hot tea even when he came in a little late. She had even brought a mug for him from home. He did not understand what she saw in him. He knew only too well when he walked past a mirror what he looked like! He would certainly try to keep himself a bit tidier, if only for her sake, he thought.

"You know, when you sweat, the dirt gets everywhere, and your clothes slip down," he justified himself. He wanted to say something more but was interrupted by the sound of the bell.

The girls had a last, quick look in the small mirrors of their handbags before they walked back to their workplaces.

Jim took the large broom and started sweeping the floor. He put the rubbish into bags. Soon sweat was pouring down his face again. From time to time, he looked at the girls and then carried on sweeping.

At the end of the day, he wiped his sweaty face with his girlfriend's apron, which she always left on the table, ready for the next day. Then he took her to the tram. There was a lot of pushing and jostling when it arrived. He had to use all his strength to help her get on. He felt more dead than alive as he walked to his lodgings.

He unwrapped the *chips* he had bought on the way home and poured vinegar over them. Then he went to the little cooker and put the kettle on for tea. He had his supper. Every bit of bread and every piece of potato was visible through his scrawny cheeks. He slurped his tea as he leafed through the paper (this was his only luxury; it cost him a penny every night, and tuppence on Sundays). He checked the number of *accidents* that day, read the latest football news, and looked at the pictures. Then he started reading an article about the royal family, about the duchess who was about to go into labour...but his eyes were already closing. He put the paper aside, went to bed and fell asleep immediately.

It was Sunday. On Sundays, Jim always dressed up in a plum-coloured suit. The trousers were so wide on him that they flapped around his skinny legs like petticoats. He put on a green and gold check tie, which he had bought at Woolworth's on his girlfriend's advice. He had lunch in a restaurant and afterwards he read an episode of an Edgar Wallace detective story, as well as the rest of the paper. In the evening they went to the *pictures* together, and while they were standing in the long queue for cheap tickets, they ate most of the sweets they had brought to eat during the film.

That Sunday evening Jim was finally persuaded. He was sitting next to his girl watching the screen, his arm around her waist. When the star on the screen was embraced by her lover, she looked so passionate and seductive, that it took Jim's breath away. And there he was with a warm, sweet creature in his arms... He proposed to her that very moment. They wouldn't postpone it, he said, they would get married as soon as the law permitted. And he kept his word.

The big day came and Jim had put on his best suit for the occasion. When he was about to put his signature on the wedding documents, his thin hand suddenly trembled: he remembered he was a Jew. He even saw the two flickering lights of the candles in front of him that his grandmother used to bless every Friday night. He saw his father - blessed be his memory, as his mother would say - and the pen slipped from his hand.

On Monday, they went back to work. The girls had put some money together to buy a cake. Even the boss came down to have a piece. He did not say anything about them taking half an hour for their tea break in honour of the young couple.

Jim scarcely took any part in the celebration. He replied automatically to all the words of congratulations. He kept hearing a voice in his head, saying "Jew", "*goy*", "Jew", "*goy.*" He did not know himself what he was anymore. He kept himself aloof, as if the party had nothing to do with him.

# *Breaking the Fast*

Old Borenstein came home from the slaughterhouse utterly exhausted. He had been wiping his knife all day long, sliding it past his thumbnail and over the plucked necks of the chickens. The boys had not given him any breathing space. They kept on at him all the time:

*"Come on,* Reb Borenstein, *come on, hurry up!"*

He had hardly emptied one crate of birds, before they shoved another one in his direction. His fingers were smeared with blood. He barely had the strength to keep pushing the chicken heads through the holes in the table next to him. His white coat had turned bright red. His rolled-up sleeves were encrusted with blood. Small beads of condensation ran down the low dividing walls. The boys were happily smothered in feathers. Mr Borenstein's face was covered in perspiration. The shrieks of the chickens were driving him mad. And as if that were not enough, there was the racket of the market outside, in the *Lane*.

The women had descended on the *Lane* like locusts, looking for bargains. But the chicken sellers were not in the mood to give anything away that day. After all, it was Yom Kippur, the Day of Atonement, when everyone was preparing for the fast, and it was only once a year! They chased the women away and would not allow them to pick their own birds. The saleswomen made such a row, you would think they themselves were being slaughtered, and if a particularly stubborn Jewish woman insisted on checking out one of the birds for herself, she could expect a slap on her wrist.

The commotion went on until late into the night. The special prayerbooks for Yom Kippur were selling fast.

"Come and buy, Jews! Buy here, it's dirt cheap, Jews! *Grapes!* Don't forget to fast! Yom Kippur candles! Parsley! Jews! Jews!"

Old Borenstein was completely deaf by then, but the stalls outside were still buzzing with excitement. The chickens looked almost green in the strange, flickering light of the lamps, as they shone on the intestines, gizzards and livers. Dark shadows were playing on the flustered faces of the saleswomen, giving them a ghostly look.

The blood. The voices. The heavy work. It had all been too much for him. When he came home, he could still hear the screams echoing in his quiet room. He immediately got undressed. He could not stop yawning while he said his evening prayers. Then he went to bed.

But he was too tired to sleep. He started thinking about Yom Kippur, the year before, how he had come home even more tired than now - so tired that he had thrown himself on the bed still dressed in his bloodstained clothes.

He had woken up late that day, he remembered. He had only just managed to find a *minyan*, a quorum of ten men, also latecomers, with whom to say prayers. When he came back the flat had already been beautifully arranged for the occasion. Everything had looked so festive. His wife had made several tasty dishes from the chicken. He hadn't wanted to stop eating. Then night fell; they finished their meal. The table had been covered with a sparkling white cloth. In the high, silver candlesticks four small, blue flames were leaping towards the ceiling. A light flickered in the middle of the table, in a thick, glass candle-holder covered with greasy fingerprints.

She had been alive. She was standing over the candles and with both hands covering her face she had softly poured out her heart to God in heaven. He had prepared himself to go out, wrapping up his prayer shawl and the prayer book for the High Holy day. He had waited for her to finish blessing the candles, so that they could go to the synagogue together that evening for *Kol Nidre*, the first service of Yom Kippur.

Now he was twisting and turning in bed like a werewolf. It was no good to be alone. No good. No good at all!

After a sleepless night he got up late. Again, he barely managed to find a *minyan*. On his way out to the prayers, he heard the *landlady* from downstairs chattering to her cat.

She was giving the cat a kiss right on its mouth. At the same time he heard a man laughing like an idiot.

It was his neighbour on the second floor. He spent whole days downstairs because he did not get along with his wife. She used to work in a factory, and all she had ever done was roam the streets with the other factory girls. There were two things she enjoyed - going to the cinema  and powdering her nose. She did not care much about religion. Although she was a Christian, she never went to church. She even cleaned the rooms on Sundays. He, on the other hand, was the son of a Christian mother and a Jewish father. He was very pious, a devout Gentile and he went to church every week. He observed all the Protestant laws as strictly as possible. He had even joined the Salvation Army in an attempt to atone for the sin of having a Jewish father. Whenever his wife shouted at him, he would find refuge downstairs with his friend, the *landlady*.

His wife was always nagging him about spending too much money on things she considered ridiculous, such as a hat with a stiff brim, embroidered with gold letters, which was part of his Salvation Army uniform. Yesterday he had been even more extravagant. He had bought himself a blue coat with epaulettes like a general. He had spent a fortune, and so now he sat downstairs with Mrs Stone.

She understood him, Mrs Stone. She was a plump Jewish woman with long, grey, curly hair. She had a fleshy, wrinkled neck and a hard face  the colour of wine. Though her eyes bulged slightly, they still had a twinkle in them which was unusually lively for a seventy-year-old. Over the years she had had many different *tenants* there, but none was as nice as Mr Davies.

She had lived in the house for over forty years. She had buried her husband there, as well as her old father, and at least two dozen cats. Now there was nothing left for her to do but look after herself and the cat, and therefore Mr Davies was a most welcome visitor. She could tell him all her problems, how she simply couldn't stand that butcher on the second  floor, for instance. Recently, another disaster had struck, the way they were making a complete mess of her wonderful neighbourhood. She complained: *"Isn't it a crime, Mr Davies? Have you seen what they are doing!"*

Mr Davies understood her very well. They were sitting in a long, dark room, in wicker armchairs with faded cushions. Opposite him there was a framed picture of two dogs and a cat hanging on the wall. Next to it there was another picture of Mrs Stone's parents, and then there was a large portrait of Mrs Stone herself.

Mr Davies blinked his Jewish eyes as he softly stroked the cat's rough, black fur. He was a willing contributor to Mrs Stone's lamentations. He told her how on a beautiful summer day, when the sun was hovering like a piece of old gold over the large front gardens and beautiful flowers, he had seen a group of tanned and muscled non-Jews arrive in their neighbourhood. They had come to demolish perfectly elegant, white stucco houses and their fine, brass door-knockers. Bang! Bang! Bang!

Polished doors and windows had fallen. Old, well-built houses, like hers, had been destroyed. They had erected a white fence around the site, and in less than a year they had replaced the houses with a whole row of shiny, brick-red tenement buildings. Instead of nannies in their smart blue cloaks, the only thing you could see now was the children being let out on a leather leash, like dogs. There was nowhere for them to let off steam. They had to spend their whole time inside the tenement buildings.

*"I wish 'he' would move there!"* she waved her plump old hand in the general direction of the second floor. "The whole of September he has been making *noise* with that ram's horn of his: 'Tra-traaaa, tkuk-koooo'." As she imitated old Borenstein, she grew even redder in the face, thoroughly enjoying her own joke. It reminded her of another one of his misdeeds.

"Do you remember," she asked Mr Davies, "the infernal racket they made, when his wife died? It was a *disgrace!*"

Earlier that morning, Mrs Stone had treated herself to roast chicken, instead of her usual breakfast of *bacon and eggs*, to celebrate Yom Kippur. She had bought the chicken in a non-kosher shop. Now Fred Davies was going to drive her to the liberal synagogue. She was all dressed up with long, dangling earrings. She carried an English version of the prayer book with her in a small, leather suitcase.

When she came home, there was a card waiting on her doormat, wishing her a "Happy New Year". It was from the Davies family. She was so touched, she could not stop looking at the card, at the purple flowers and the golden, embroidered *Shana Tova*, New Year greeting which she could not read as she did not understand Hebrew. Instead she read the English inscription, which brought tears to her eyes.

Old Borenstein came home in the evening, tired after a whole day of fasting and praying and blowing the ram's horn. He had carried back his prayer shawl, his slippers and the Yom Kippur drops which he had sprinkled on his handkerchief to help him keep alert during the service. He walked up the dark stairs very slowly. He lit two candles. He could see the dark blue night sky through the windows and could hear people walking by downstairs, Jews who were coming back from the synagogue, wishing each other all the best for the coming year.

Mrs Stone downstairs and Mr Borenstein upstairs. Both of them were sitting on their own, breaking the fast...

# *Becoming a Tramp*

Bill rolled his sleeves down. His long, stick-like arms were covered in thick, green veins. He beat the flecks of flour off his old jacket until it became dark again.

For the past eight years, he had had to change jobs many times and not out of choice. If it had been up to him, he would have liked to stay in his current position for the last few years he had left. But, of course, nobody ever asked him what he wanted. It was always the same: just as he was getting used to a place, to the job and the people, there would be a hitch - and he would be asked to leave.

This time he was working in a bakery. They were good people. He earned two pounds and ten shillings a week. They always paid him on time, and he was never bullied.

The baker's wife, a buxom Jewish woman with a wide parting in her thin, grey hair and a round, smiling face, treated him like a son. Every morning before he went home after a long night's work, she would put a paper bag full of bagels in his hands: "So, Bill, today at least you'll have a nice, Jewish *breakfast*," she would beam with pleasure, and all the warts on her flabby cheeks and chin would smile in unison.

The baker himself was a short Jew with a floury beard, who never stopped threatening his workers that he would send them home, all of them, saying that he didn't need any "union shmunion" people in his bakery. In spite of that, most of them had worked for him for at least ten or fifteen years. So it was a real shame that he had to give Bill the sack.

One day, one of the workers, a tall boy with broad shoulders who had started work at the age of fourteen when he left school, and who was already a father, imitated the baker:

"I don't need any 'union shmunion' people! This is a bakery, not a union!" he said with an angry voice, while trying to appear shorter than he was. Everybody had been in stitches and Bill felt at home.

Today, the boys each slipped a shilling into his hand and looked at him sadly.

"What do you think you're going to do, Bill?" one of them asked. Bill turned around in surprise. Ever since he had started working there, nobody had called him by his name, except for the baker's wife. When he had arrived in the bakery six months earlier, the boys had taken one look at him and decided to call him a *shlemiel*, he was such a wretched, simple creature.

The skin on Bill's finely etched cheekbones was dark and thin. The lines on his low forehead appeared to have been drawn by a knife dipped in black ink. Dirt filled the nails on his long, bony fingers. His eyes were bloodshot and watery. Then there were Bill's clothes - the jacket he wore each and every day was shapeless and threadbare. It had got so thin in places you could see his bones. The jacket made his elongated body look even skinnier. He looked like a dead tramp that still had a smile on his face. It was a brooding smile.

The baker paid Bill an extra week's wages, and said apologetically to his wife, "What can I do, when the customers stay away? They are disgusted by him!"

His wife wrapped up a small piece of bread in the meantime, and added a few biscuits that had gone soft: "Here, Bill, for the children!"

Bill had left the shop quickly. It was full of light and sunshine. Everything in it exuded an air of plenty. The baker's wife followed him with her eyes and shook her head: "If only he would have kept himself a bit cleaner..."

"Don't talk nonsense!" the baker said, as he arranged the cakes on a tray. He then told his wife why Bill did not keep himself 'a bit cleaner'.

"You know, he's got tuberculosis, and his wife won't let him into the house. He doesn't even have a place to shave. Did you see his chin? It's so sharp and bristly. Just like a black pig.

"He insisted on fighting in the war, our hero. Well, he's paid a heavy price. And who is going to help him? Poor sod. Who is going to employ a man whose lungs have been shot to pieces? *They* won't, for sure! He can still get a job with one of us for a few weeks. But with them? It is a fact, Bill offered to mow the lawn of the lady with the big garden, and she just slammed the door in his face. She wouldn't even talk to him. Apparently, she said to her servant - the one with the blue dress who wears a stiff, white cap on her grey hair - that his mouth 'was as empty as a grave' and she was disgusted he was so dirty."

The baker's wife, who had been tut-tutting as her husband spoke, rejoined: "That's how they are. They don't know anything about compassion. For them, if you have money, you're lucky. If you don't, you can start digging your own grave."

"It was Mrs Levy, that lady's neighbour, who convinced me at the time to give him a job in the bakery. She said she knew him. 'He is an honest fellow and he deserves a chance,' she told me. That's why I took him on. But I can't lose customers because of him, can I?"

Bill did not have any desire to go home. He knew the look his wife would give him. It would make him feel hot and cold at the same time. He would start coughing up blood, and then there would be nothing else to do but slink away again. So he walked to a nearby park.

It was a sunny day. The array of well-kept flowerbeds made for a dazzling, colourful display and there was a lovely fresh smell in the air.

Children were screaming and laughing as they rolled on the grass. Dogs frolicked around and barked loudly with pleasure. Couples were lying in each other's arms, forgetting that they might be needed at work. Loving each other on the grass meant they would not get any money at the end of the week.

"There is no work," they said to each other, "but there is sunshine! And when do we get any sun here?" They decided to live for the moment.

On a separate piece of freshly cut grass a group of about ten elderly men were bowling. They stood there slightly bent, with serious faces, their grey eyes transfixed. They followed the black balls with intense curiosity as they rolled smoothly over the grass.

Their wives were sitting on two wooden benches nearby - shrivelled old women in dark clothes with pious faces and big hats on their grey heads. They looked at the game. Some of them were knitting waistcoats.

The Jewish women were sitting a bit further on. They were having a chat about cooking and baking, and Jewish troubles. They were also amused to see how seriously the old people took their game.

"That's a clever game they're playing there, isn't it?" they said, shaking their heads in a mocking fashion.

"Absolutely. Just imagine a Jew going bowling!"

Bill sat there a couple of hours watching the black balls on the green grass. From time to time, he really got involved in the play, wondering whether the ball would hit the target or not. Finally, he went home.

His four boys were sitting in the kitchen, on a clean rug, which was torn in places. They were busy building a 'palace'. They even had a pennant, stuck between the wooden blocks. All four of them had the same granite grey eyes and they looked well-fed with healthy red cheeks.

When they saw their father, they were very pleased, not so much because of him, but because now they had a chance to show him what a fine palace they had built.

"You see, daddy," the middle one said ecstatically, "that's what Mr Brown has bought for us. He says that he will buy us a real palace if we don't cry when mummy goes away."

Bill smiled sourly.

"So, he's a good man, is he, that Mr Brown?" he asked his eldest, who was eight years old. With a cheerful "yes" on the tip of his tongue, the little one suddenly saw how his father was looking at him. The words stuck in his throat and he stopped talking. Without understanding why, he frantically started to pile up the blocks higher and higher. Then, with a sudden gesture, he destroyed the whole edifice. The wooden blocks shot out in all directions - and the word "yes" lingered on in the air.

"Where is your mother?" Bill asked the children angrily.

They did not answer.

"Where is your mother?" he coughed.

"Mummy has said that I should say that I don't know," the four-year-old said. The oldest boy giggled. He shut up immediately and started collecting the wooden blocks from the floor.

"Mummy has gone away with Mr Brown. He said that if she didn't go with him she would have to pay the rent again," the oldest boy said softly, as if telling his father a secret.

"You won't tell her that I've told you, will you?" the little one asked, wanting reassurance.

"Not tell her!" Bill muttered under his breath.

"Not Mr Brown either!" the six-year-old called out abruptly. He was a plump boy with blond hair and a snotty nose, his little hands full of the blocks he was picking up from the floor. "Otherwise he will not buy the palace," he said, explaining the logic to Bill.

Bill left. He went back into the park. He took a seat on a bench next to a lake. A blue-winged duck was swimming in the water, followed by a dozen yellow ducklings.

Bill threw the soggy biscuits in the water. The duck swam straight at them, together with all her ducklings. He watched how greedily they nibbled away at the biscuits.

A shabby old man with an overgrown grey beard, long, tousled hair and a pair of worn-out shoes which revealed all ten naked, swollen toes on his cracked feet, sat himself down with a heavy sigh.

"Hello, Bill! Are we having another holiday?"

Bill looked straight through the old man. His thoughts were very far away.

"She was once a really decent woman, I can tell you," he said to himself while he stared fixedly ahead.

"What do you mean?" The old man looked at Bill with sickly, bulging eyes; he thought Bill had been talking to him.

"He has taken her away from me for the rent and the children's food."

The old man had no clue what he was talking about.

Night fell. It was not long before they heard the sound of a bell and the voice of the park keeper calling "everybody out!". Bill, who was still holding a small piece of bread, left the park together with the old man to look for a place to spend the night.

They settled down on the stone steps of a tobacco factory. They shared the bread the baker's wife had given Bill and the old man's rags.

Bill had become a tramp.

# Too Late

The Segals are preparing themselves for a big party in their home. They are expecting a very important guest from abroad.

All the lights are burning in the enormous, crystal chandelier. Even the little lamps on the embossed wallpaper, normally merely decorative, have been switched on today, throwing their long shadows on the walls opposite and onto the deep yellow Persian rug. The long room is bathed in a sea of light. The crystal vases and bowls on the sideboard are caught in a sparkling dance of green, red, yellow, and white. The colours leap up like flames, chasing each other and bouncing off the oval mirror opposite.

The heavy, shining mahogany table has been pulled out to its full length. Fine pieces of silver are displayed in a glass case near the table. In a picture above the mantelpiece Shirley, the eldest daughter, observes everything with a smile on her face. It looks as if she could step out of the picture at any moment, and take a seat at the long table, while the frame would remain there, empty and forlorn, above the marble mantelpiece. The parquet floor surrounding the carpet gleams like a mirror. It has been polished to the point of danger.

A love scene between Greek gods is unfolding on the small carpet in front of the mantelpiece. Shirley looks down on them with some amusement, but without the slightest intention of leaving her frame.

The cook is sweating. She has been standing on her swollen feet since early that morning, and she is still not ready. She keeps on cooking and frying, roasting and baking: there is chopped fish and fried fish, chicken soup and roasted duck, meat loaf and rolled veal, cake and all kinds of *puddings*, *apple pie*, and strudel - a combination of Jewish home cooking and authentic

English dishes. She has even thought of making *Yorkshire pudding*.

Mrs Segal has become English through and through. She knows that it is correct to say *"I haven't done it,"* rather than *"I didn't done it."* She laughs at *foreigners*, and keeps herself to herself. She even has a little dog, which she takes out on a leash when she goes to buy fish and chicken and expensive fruit, which is later brought to her door by poor Jewish or, as is more often the case, non-Jewish delivery boys.

With true Jewish pride she always gives the *goyim* a larger tip, so as not to make anti-Semites out of them.

And of course, she keeps up Jewish traditions. She lights the candles every Friday night and places them carefully in the front room. She turns on all the lights in the room and never closes the heavy, plush curtains. She is not ashamed - on the contrary, she is proud to be Jewish. She derives great pleasure from watching the *goyim* stand there gawping outside her windows. She loves to see the look of amazement on their faces when they notice the large, luxurious room where the heavy, silver Sabbath candlesticks spread an air of festiveness.

The imminent arrival of a visitor is causing a great stir in the household, not least of all because there are three daughters in this house, and the guest is a cousin of theirs. They also know that he is no ordinary young man. He has a university degree. In fact, he has just become a doctor. The brother-in-law of Mrs Segal, her sister's husband, has written to them to say that his son has not simply graduated, oh no, he has received the highest distinction. His professor has advised him strongly not to let himself be led astray, which happens to so many young doctors: on no account should he open a "shop"; he has to continue his studies and become an eye specialist. Therefore, he asks them, the Segals, to help his son make his dreams come true.

Mrs Segal does not really understand what he means by the word "shop". What she does know, however, is that her brother-in-law is a learned Jew, not like her Jack, and even though he is very poor, he has encouraged all his children to study. Apart from his son, who will arrive any minute now, he also has two girls who go to good schools, which she in fact pays for. She knows that if it were not for her generosity, they would just die of hunger.

Mr Segal paces back and forth in the large room in eager anticipation of his guest. In order to make time pass more quickly, he stands still every once in a while next to his daughters, who are sitting on the sofa and in the large armchairs. The girls are petite and slim. They are wearing short dresses that are pulled up far above their knees, revealing fine legs in real silk stockings.

The small dog follows every step its master makes, and it pauses whenever he does. It snorts through its little black nose with happiness because everybody is there in the room and he is there with them.

Mr Segal takes in everything in the room and, to his own surprise, he realises for the first time how pretty his daughters are.

He takes a look in the mirror, and he sees that he himself is still looking good and young for his age. When he peeks at his wife, he wonders how it is possible that he has not noticed how much weight she has put on. Her bosom has become enormous. Her hips are large, her shoulders broad. There are grey streaks in her hair.

It seems to him as if all this has happened overnight. They have lived together for thirty years now and he has never noticed any changes. She always looked the same, he thought. Only now does he remember his wife's constant complaining: that she is getting too fat, that after every childbirth her *varicose veins* are getting worse and her feet more swollen, practically bursting out of her shoes.

Is she, this woman with the three double chins, with the bright, chubby face and the tiny, deep-set eyes - is she the same Hannah, the girl with the long face, full of character and the sharp, protruding chin? Is she the one with the big, blue eyes, the girl he had to fight a battle to win? His girl, who blames him each and every day that he cheated her. She thought that he was an intellectual in that *shtetl* of his, but soon after fleeing to London together, it turned out he was nothing more than an ordinary tailor.

"Ha, ha, ha!" he laughs, "was she really worth fighting for?"

His wife scrutinises him with her piggy eyes. She does not have any idea what he is thinking about.

"Did you say something, Jack?"

"No. Nothing! *It's all right.*"

He looks at their wedding picture, which stands on a small table in the corner, and then at himself again. He has to admit that he has changed quite a bit himself as well. He takes off the square *yarmulke*, which he has worn the whole day, revealing a gleaming, white patch. All that is left from the fine thatch of brown hair in the picture is a silver rim. It disturbs him to discover that he is already grey too, or rather, that he is even greyer than she is. And the longish, slightly bent nose has become a lot fleshier, thicker and rounder. He turns away from the mirror and puts the *yarmulke* back on his head.

"None of us is getting any younger."

He looks at his hairy wrist with the broad leather band. His watch tells him that it is half past five.

"It's getting late. He has to be taken to the synagogue," he says to his eldest daughter, who is leaning close to the radio listening to a symphony.

*"I suppose they will soon be here."* She does her best to sound casual. She does not want her father to know that she is at all interested in seeing her cousin, whom everybody in this room already considers - without speaking about it and without the boy's consent - the future son-in-law.

The grey car, which was sent to the station an hour ago to pick him up, arrives with a roaring noise.

The trees in the small front garden, their branches cut into a round shape, enjoy the golden light of dusk. The brightly coloured chrysanthemums look more beautiful than ever in the last rays of the setting sun. Just like the owner of the house, the sun seems to refuse to admit that it is past its prime.

All three daughters move simultaneously towards the bay window, careful to keep behind the tulle curtains. They do not want the guest to know how curious they are.

Mr Segal himself adjusts his *yarmulke* and he walks outside in a light-hearted fashion to welcome his wife's nephew.

Mrs Segal remains in the doorway. She is standing there, her face beaming, holding her plump arms wide open, ready to swallow him up in her embrace, tall as he is, and to cover him with kisses.

It has been thirty years since she left her home. In a flash she sees her *shtetl*, and herself as a young girl, her whole family waiting for her, also with wide-open arms. A tear rolls down her right cheek.

A man jumps deftly out of the car. It's Harry, the Segals' only son: blond, portly, dressed in a bright suit and white shoes. He stands next to the door of the car, smiling, waiting for his cousin to come out. When he sees the little dog, he picks it up and starts talking to it.

Emerging from the car behind him is a rather gloomy man, about thirty years old, who is wearing a crumpled grey suit and a pair of worn shoes. He looks extremely worried. His dark brown eyes have a hungry glint.

The girls exclaim in unison: "Oooh!" They return to their armchairs and make themselves comfortable. They really could not care less what they look like.

In the meantime, Mr Segal takes the young man by the arm and introduces him with great ceremony to his aunt.

Mrs Segal has turned pale; she has completely forgotten that she has to kiss her nephew. When she remembers, she just kisses his forehead. Her dream has been shattered. Her entire past has been erased in one single moment.

Mr Segal almost stumbles over his wife as he tries to get past her, holding his guest by the hand. She just stands there on the doorstep, paralysed. He has no idea what is wrong with her.

He introduces the guest to his eldest daughter. All three girls jump up at once. Extending their slender hands, they ask politely, *"How do you do?"* They try very hard not to burst out laughing when this man in his shabby shoes takes the hand of each one of them, brings it to his lips and kisses the long, red fingernails. He then answers back softly and with quiet confidence: *"How do you do?"* He sounds like a born Englishman. They stare at him in amazement:

"Huh! What's this?"

The servant girl, who is wearing a bright blue blouse and a black satin skirt in honour of the guest, brings in tea.

With great dexterity the young man holds the fine porcelain cup in one hand, the plate in the other. He even calls it *"a cup of tea"*. He does not seem at all uncomfortable. He enjoys the delicacies he is being offered from all sides. If anything, he is the one who is smiling sarcastically, at the girls' lack of sophistication.

Later on, Harry shows him the bathroom. A white stove burns pleasantly in there and a shiny black bathtub, almost filled to the rim, is waiting for him invitingly. But when he catches sight of himself in the full-length mirror, he starts feeling less sure of himself.

Next to the little rubber mat right beside the bath, there is a real carpet, a black one, with a bunch of yellow tulips woven artfully into the pattern. They almost look real in the soft glow of the dying sunlight.

Mr Segal tactfully brings in a fresh set of underwear and socks, a suit and a pair of shoes. He begs his nephew to try on the clothes, since he gathers that something must have happened to his luggage along the way.

The young man turns red and starts stuttering: "Eh, yes... I mean..."

But Mr Segal interrupts his nephew's search for an excuse.

"*Please, hurry up.* We have to go to the synagogue quite soon." He walks out of the bathroom, relieved to leave his nephew there.

The young man looks bemused: "Synagogue Jews, really? Oh yes," he now remembers the *yarmulke* his uncle is wearing. "What a curious country!"

The clothes fit him perfectly. Mr Segal has sewn the garments himself by guessing the measurements of his nephew with the help of a picture. Mr Segal has always had an eye for these things. He still loves to sit down amidst the workers in his factory and show his master tailor how to do a particularly difficult piece of work.

He places a shiny top hat on his round head. He is wearing a black dress-coat and a pair of pressed, pinstripe trousers. A pair of brown leather gloves complete his outfit. He puts the small, dark-red *tallis* bag, where he keeps his prayer shawl, under his arm, and Mr Segal is ready to go. Harry has replaced his white shoes with brown ones. His soft, grey hat askew, he is playing with the dog again. When Mrs Segal has finished blessing the candles, they all go to the synagogue.

The synagogue is suffused with light. The chandeliers send glittering rays down from the ceiling.

Jews are coming to meet him. Almost all of them are corpulent men with big bellies, top hats and smiles on their faces. They greet him and want to know how life is in "the old country". Some used to know his father. One of them, the heaviest of them all, with the biggest diamond pin in the broadest tie, says he remembers him from there; they used to go to *cheder* together. He tells him that when he was about to start at the academy, his parents had taken him to London.

"And here we are!" He is clearly very pleased with himself.

The guest does not believe his eyes: this large Jew, with his ostentatious tiepin, who looks more like a pig farmer than anything else, was the neighbour's ten-year-old son? Wasn't he the one all the other boys made fun of, because he was always going around in torn trousers that had become too small for him? But this man looks fifteen years older than him! And yet, when he takes a good look at him, he does indeed see similarities. Yes, it's him.

"I've heard that you have become a doctor. You always were clever. I was never any good at Hebrew. *But I don't really care, believe me!*" The man has lapsed into English, forgetting that he is talking to a newcomer. "After all, I've got twelve butcher shops now," he says proudly.

"*I am very pleased to hear that,*" the "newcomer" answers him, in perfect English.

"What? So you don't come from the old country then?" A cloud of disappointment spreads over their round faces.

"I most certainly do," the guest comforts them. "People study English there as well, you know."

"They study there better than anywhere else," Mr Segal says with satisfaction, and Harry laughs, then says in English: "*I think he'll give you all a lesson in English, ha–ha–ha!*"

They start praying. Harry sways above his prayer book and looks up. He counts the red and blue panes in the tall windows of the synagogue. The building used to be a church, which the Jews have bought and rebuilt.

Back at home, Mr Segal says the blessing over the wine; he muddles up all the words. It does not matter to him because on this special occasion he feels like doing it by heart. His nephew has to bite his lips not to laugh.

The food is spectacular, though. Never in his life has he eaten dishes such as these; they look irresistible. The young man hesitates: he has no idea what one is supposed to do with the mountain of plates and endless rows of knives, forks and spoons. But he watches his cousins closely. He imitates every movement of his uncle who turns out to be an expert, and thus he manages not to make a single gaffe.

The girls hardly ever see their cousin. His days are spent elsewhere and in the evening he sits at his desk, red-eyed and surrounded by heavy books. He has no time for them.

The girls are rarely at home anyway. They play tennis all day long, they swim or they go off to Bournemouth. Sometimes they stroll in the West End and look at the shop windows. In winter they go to *charity* concerts. At night they are out dancing. In fact, they just don't care about their cousin and his affairs, especially now that he seems to be getting more and more involved in that eye research of his. Even the clothes, handmade by their father, look baggy on him, and his eyes are getting redder every day from studying at night.

Mr and Mrs Segal are becoming nervous. They are afraid that their daughters will go off with other men and leave their cousin to his own devices. The parents would much rather have him, a relative, as their son-in-law, especially now that he is about to start his own practice in Harley Street and become a *specialist*.

"Listen to me, you have to ask him how much longer he's going to study." Every night Mrs Segal nags her husband while both of them are lying awake in bed. "He could be a specialist already. But he doesn't know you are ready to help him set up the business. The other day you had the perfect opportunity. You know, when he was saying that specialists nowadays have machines at home with which they can see what's going on in their patients' eyes. It would have been so easy, if only you were not such a *fool*, to tell him then and there that you will arrange for him to have such a machine. Then you would have had a nice talk and you could have told him that it's time to start thinking about marriage."

"What are you going on about? They're not even engaged, and you are talking about marriage already!"

"*Nu*, so, then we'll make an engagement!"

The couple quarrel deep into the night until they finally come to an agreement. The engagement will be announced on Sunday.

*"Well, I wish you luck!"* Mrs Segal kisses her eldest daughter, Shirley, early the following morning. The girl is sitting in her pyjamas at the *dressing table* in her smart bedroom and puts a green cream on her face.

*"Why?"* There is a look of amazement in Shirley's streaming eyes, in which she has put drops a moment ago to make them shine.

"*Daddy* has agreed that Sunday will be the day of your engagement to Dennis and we will rent an apartment for him on Harley Street. Enough with the studying! He should know how to do the tricks of his trade by now! Your sisters will start looking for husbands and you will become an old spinster, if we have to wait for him. He thinks to be a specialist, he has to get old first."

"And nobody has asked me anything? *I have nothing to say, or what?*" Shirley, who has a beatific smile on her face, caresses her mother's cheek affectionately. Suddenly she jumps up, grabs her mother by the waist, and dances around the room with her. Mrs Segal is huffing and puffing; she can barely follow the slim girl. Eventually she manages to free herself and she drops heavily on the silk blanket on the unmade bed.

"Do you love him?"

"Love him? *Well, I don't know. But,* you know, mother *they'll go mad* with jealousy when they find out that my fiancé is a specialist in Harley Street."

"*Of course, darling!* It's good that you understand. I've always known that you are a *practical girl.*"

Mr and Mrs Segal are sitting opposite their nephew feeling rather flustered, almost ashamed, as if they are about to commit a sin. They summon up their courage and start talking about their decision. They tell him that it is time for him to *settle*. The younger girls will not wait endlessly for Shirley, and they as parents don't want to bring shame on Shirley by allowing her sisters to get married before her, and so on and so on.

The young man's face darkens. He too has got something similar to say. He has prepared himself carefully. He has rehearsed every word many times. It's difficult, but he doesn't have a choice.

He has a girl. She is very sweet. He would do anything for her. She loves him too. She'd give her life for him. He feels that the time is right for them. His uncle has a good heart. So does his aunt. They will understand. They were young once. He even knows, his mother has told the story many times, that her sister brought shame on everybody by falling in love with a tailor and running away with him. Of all the people in the world his aunt must know how it feels: to be apart from the person one cares about most in the whole world, and not to be able to bring her over because of a few lousy pounds.

They will surely help him. He hasn't done anything wrong, apart from being a fool, a naughty little boy. He should have talked to them earlier, that's true. But, at least he knows now that very soon he will be able to pay them back, bit by bit, for everything they have done for him. When he has a *flat*, he will be able to live lawfully together with his wife. They must be pleased about that. And how wonderful it will be for him, and for his girl especially, not to have to live with this terrible yearning any longer.

"You impudent rascal!" Mrs Segal bangs on the table. She tries to hold back the tears with all her might, but she can't. She weeps like a little girl.

"What will Shirley say?" she sobs.

Shirley laughs as she wipes away the tears from her mother's face. She keeps telling her that she wouldn't have wanted him anyway. She never really liked him in the first place. He's such a bore.

*"She can have him!"* she calls out cheerfully, and she walks upstairs to her room, hiding her own tears.

# Two Libraries

Light pours into the library's large anteroom with its green, shiny walls. Thick, smooth columns support the finely vaulted ceiling. The red and white tiled floor is cold and clean, except for a small puddle of muddy water by the door. A long bench is crammed with the old and the young - elderly men and women who have sat down for a moment to pause for breath, and small children waiting for their parents who have gone in to pick up books. Above the bench, warning notices sternly caution the public:

Smoking Is Strictly Forbidden.

No Spitting. Offenders Will Be Prosecuted.

A pillory stands right next to the window, a permanent reminder! An inscription is carved in this instrument of torture, with an explanation for the viewer about past forms of punishment. Back in olden days, when mankind was not yet civilised, the sinners would have been wedged onto the pillory, in the middle of the marketplace, so upright citizens could come and do good deeds by throwing rotten eggs and rubbish at them. The really pious would throw stones as well. Most often, the sinner died of shame and anguish.

It is Friday evening. The anteroom is bustling with people walking in and out. One would expect to find the young girls and boys, who are coming in to exchange books, in dance halls or cinemas, rather than in here. Yet they take two, three books at a time! Some of the boys are dressed in short trousers, revealing bare knees. All kinds of hikers and cyclists are walking in, accompanied by girls with broad, mannish shoes and hair cut short, like a boy. One also sees many young Jewish faces. Old, Gentile women are entering with large Victorian hats towering over their pointed faces. The husbands have watery eyes and small, bony faces, an extinguished pipe in their toothless mouths.

Little schoolboys are dashing in with red cheeks and mischievous eyes, followed by fresh young girls in high-heeled shoes. Housewives, baskets in hand, are hurrying in after them. Even pregnant women come here to have a good read.

Inside, in the big hall with the overfilled shelves, there is a big rush on Edgar Wallace. Old women take out Mrs Henry Wood - you can shed a pleasurable tear over *East Lynne*. The hikers, cyclists, and girls with short hair try a book in translation once in a while. People make their way through the library like a dense forest, not knowing where it begins or where it will end.

Lithe girls with manicured nails and painted lips bring in yet more piles of books. Their weight almost crushes them. It looks as if these lovely, slim bodies might snap in two at any moment and the heavy books will all end up on the floor of the library, uncovered, ashamed of their nakedness. But the girls are used to doing their job. They place the books where they belong with great care and the next moment they are whirling through the long, shiny hall again, ready to pick up a new load.

The girls at the entrance and exit doors also have their hands full. Books need to be stamped, dates have to be filled in, and baskets, which are not allowed in the library, have to be taken from their owners, ostensibly out of respect for the printed word, but possibly also for another reason.

The whole place is brimming with life!

The Jewish library is an entirely different world.

The counter stands in a long hall as a dividing line between the reading room and the lending library.

Elderly Jews come here, not so much to borrow books, but to have a nap or a chat, to meet up with an acquaintance, to have a look at the papers. The girl at the counter does not have much to do. So she sits and knits the whole day. Knits and yawns. Yawns and knits. Jews tell stories in here, they talk about the torture chambers in Germany compared to which the pillory is a toy. They say that Jews are tormented in concentration camps, in old and more modern ways. They talk and sigh. Then they switch to Poland and tell each other stories about the plight of the Polish Jews. "What a miracle he has not invaded England. Thank God!" They start discussing anti-Semitism in general. In the end the yawns of the girl behind the counter become catching and people think it must be time to go home.

The hall gradually empties.

The small gentleman with the black eyes, dressed in a shabby, fur coat, a briefcase under his arm, has gone through almost all the foreign papers. He has also had a look at the literary magazine. He pulls a miserable face. An old man, a chicken plucker on the *Lane*, has finished reading the gripping feuilletons in the daily paper. He flicks through a magazine, mumbles something to himself about it being incomprehensible, and leaves. A Hebrew teacher, who is almost collapsing under his own excessive weight, has read out all of his poems to a suffering, hungry writer. The teacher is still basking in the beauty of his own creativity, when he realises that his only listeners are the walls. In the meantime, the writer has managed to borrow a shilling from someone and has sneaked out to get something to eat. The teacher is so angry that he soon leaves as well.

The girl at the counter has become lazy because she does not have enough to do. Sometimes she does not even bother to put away the few books that have come in.

Her only break comes in the form of a bookseller who, as a sideline, supplies her with excellent Yiddish books that could be a great success among the non-Jews too, if only they could read them. By some miracle, he manages to sell her a few books.

The librarian herself is no expert in these matters. She does not really know any Yiddish, so she purchases the best Yiddish literature along with sentimental novels. She has up to two or three times as many of the latter. If she likes the cover, she buys the book. The library is not short on funding in any case.

But when the bookseller has left as well, and her hands are sore from too much knitting, she suddenly becomes upset. She shouts at the few remaining souls that sit dreaming at their tables, their heads resting on their elbows:

"Be quiet!"

They wake up, rubbing the sleep out of their eyes. They look around at each other in the gloom...and start talking.

# She is Not Blind

The small house stands on its own, completely isolated. The houses on either side have been reduced to high piles of burned, crumbling bricks, broken, rickety furniture, and the charred remains of enormous black beams. All kinds of tools and appliances are lying around amidst endless mountains of broken glass. Inside the house, destruction weaves its silent web, just like the cobwebs appearing between the flowers and the grasses, which have sprung up wild and free among the ruins.

No one has had the courage to tear the finely woven labour of thousands of drunken spiders. No one has dared to pick the high, violet-coloured flowers, which might have adorned a table or a sideboard in a poor man's house. No one even comes near them.

The house itself has subsided somewhat. In the window, different creams, soaps, powders, and perfume bottles are on display. Two mannequins made out of wax stand at either end. One is blond and wide-eyed, with a white, almost transparent neck. Her big blue eyes have black, curled eyelashes and the eyelids are covered with glittering blue shadow. Her golden hair is glossy and her nose small and haughty. The long curls are tumbling down her comely shoulders, falling onto the small, pale, half-naked breasts. The other one is dark, with a mass of black, shiny hair, which is held up high in a bun by a large comb set with glittering stones. Her pitch-black eyes are incandescent and suggest rich, exuberant laughter. Her dark breasts, full and pert, are half covered with red satin. Various brochures are lying at their feet, full of advice about what you should do to look as gorgeous as the two wax beauties. Beads surround them - red, blue, white, amber - every colour and shape. There are brooches, parasols, and even cigarettes. Everything is covered with a film of dust.

The display window is so low that it hardly stands out above the pavement. You have to bend down very low in order to enter.

Inside the owner is dressed in a dazzling white coat, just like a doctor. The trousers that stick out from under his coat have the smoothest of creases. His brown leather shoes shine, the satin shirt is an immaculate white, and his broad, red tie hangs in a perfect knot. The blond rim around his pinkish bald pate has a veritable gleam to it. He looks pleased with himself and the world.

He is bending over a large man who lies in a high, reclining chair with soap all over his face and a white napkin tied around his neck, as if he were a small child being fed by his mother. The proprietor, Berl Melzer, feeds him all kinds of stories, which he has invented especially for him, or he talks about politics.

Mr Melzer is flanked by young men dressed in white jackets like waiters, who tower above the clients that are sitting down all over the place. Some of them have been soaped and are ready to be shaved by the boys in the short white jackets. Others are being cut in a whirlwind of dancing scissors and smoothing combs while the boys eagerly tell their stories, stories about anything and everything. They could even teach the women upstairs a lesson or two.

The customers often know more about what's going on than the boys can tell them. They were also at the dog races, or the horseracing, or at the football match, and it is quite impossible to tell them anything new.

Many of the clients are sitting on the long, worn-out plush bench opposite the high chairs. They look at their reflection in the mirrors that are covered in soap specks, and wait patiently for the proprietor.

They all want to be seen just by him, although he has so much work to do that they often wait in vain. But if a customer manages to get a seat next to the chair where Mr Melzer is already busy washing or powdering someone, then he can sneak into the chair while it is still warm, and then he too has the privilege of being cut or shaved by the boss.

The stories that he tells them are very colourful indeed, and all of them are made up from what he observes.

*"He is a jolly clever man, that Mr Melzer,"* the customers say. "When he tells you a *story*, you think that you have seen it all with your very own eyes.

Sometimes it even seems as if what he tells you has happened to you."

He is well known all over the city, and all the Jews come to him for a haircut, even those living in rich neighbourhoods, where they have to look elegant in order to fit in with their smart surroundings. They would rather go a day without a shave or a week without a haircut, just to be able to go to Mr Melzer himself and pick up a *story*. His name is celebrated, not only in his own town but in many others as well.

One day a man arrives, a writer with a bundle of books which he has printed himself and which the poor fellow now has to carry around to sell. He knows the best place for him is in this small, half-sunken house with the two dusty beauties in the less than spotless display window. And indeed, the welcome he receives is almost too much for him. The wet handshake of the boss is soft and warm - as warm as the look in his kind, smiling eyes.

All the anger and frustration caused by the lack of recognition, by people not wanting to believe that he is the greatest writer of his generation, that it should be allowed that a great man like him has to haul himself around to sell his own work, disappears. It is blown away like a cloud in the wind, and he feels a warm stream running through his body.

"How are you doing, comrade?" The writer calls Melzer comrade instead of Mister, because he knows that Melzer comes from a family of socialists, fine people.

"Please, come in. My niece, Perele, will receive you in a moment, I am terribly busy!"

Inside, in the room, which is not very big, everything is clean and pleasant. A fire is blazing in the open fireplace, even though it is summer, and it spreads a sweet, peaceful warmth over the faces of the people, and over the glowing furniture. The flames can be seen dancing in the mirror opposite and in the gleam of the radio cabinet.

Mr Melzer leaves the guest behind in the room, and he rushes back to finish a client.

Inside, Perele is busy working. She is dressed in a white coat as well. Her small face is surrounded by black hair, and she has a pair of sparkling, coal-black eyes. Her complexion is dark, her lips are red and full. She tends to pout while she is talking, and occasionally reveals a mouthful of sharp white teeth like a puppy's. The girl does not stand still for a second. She does not simply walk around the house, she runs. She does not have a moment to spare. But that does not mean she is not ready to drop everything instantly and she treats the people her uncle brings in every now and again with the greatest respect.

Before the guest has had time to count to three, a white, neatly pressed tablecloth has already appeared on the table, as well as a silver samovar with boiling-hot tea, a little jug of milk, and a pot of sugar. Tasty, thinly cut sandwiches are being piled high on a big porcelain dish and a freshly baked cake is placed upside down on a tray. Everything is beautifully laid out with great taste. Perele even places the flowers from the radio cabinet on the table in honour of the guest. She pours tea and smiles at him so warmly and charmingly that immediately he feels at home. He would love to stay there the rest of his life being waited on by "comrade" Melzer's niece; simply sitting there, endlessly watching the little one, looking at the colourful, perfumed flowers and the red, yellow and green flames dancing around in the fireplace.

"Please, just help yourself. The sandwiches are made with kosher sausages, the other ones don't have meat in them," she says, just in case the guest is vegetarian. She has thought of everything.

"Please, my uncle will be angry if you don't eat."

The guest does not need any encouragement, rather the opposite. And, while she is talking like that to the guest, she floats in the direction of her uncle. She moves her full, warm lips so close to him, one could think she is about to kiss him. What am I talking about! She is just whispering in his ear that it is time for him to eat something. She begs him to take a break and have a *cup of tea*. People can wait, even with soap on their face. She does not care.

Her uncle revels in her sweet words, but he is not coming, not yet. How can he? He is too busy! Apart from that, he does not mind if his niece comes in again to ask him a second time. He does not mind feeling her warm lips close to his burning ear once again. He knows that if he doesn't leave his customer - the man's mouth and ears wide open in eager anticipation of the rest of the story - to go inside, she will get angry with him; her brilliant black eyes will grow even darker and rounder, *sweeter than wine*. Only then will he go inside for a while, sit himself down at the table and take a sip of his tea. He will have a quick chat with the guest and pop back to work with his mouth chock-full of the biscuits that Perele will have tempted him with.

All of a sudden the guest feels a shiver running down his spine: a ghostly figure comes shuffling out of nowhere with her hands stretched out in front of her as if trying to feel her way. It seems as if she does not trust her own steps, as if she does not recognise the room. She walks as if this is the first time in her whole life she has set foot on the floorboards which, although covered, hide a deep abyss underneath the fine carpet - and there is no way back.

Looking at the apparition, he notices that her heavy, dark eyelids are lowered, and he is unable to see her eyes. He can make out her round shape and dark features. Her hair has been cut short. She has a fringe, which covers her forehead completely, all the way down to her thick, black eyebrows. Her nose is small, too small for her face. Her blue, swollen lips are dribbling.

She shuffles on regardless, all the time tapping the air around her with her small, sweaty, swollen hands. She mumbles something to herself. It looks as if she is smiling at the same time. He starts to feel uncomfortable. His lips are trembling. He wants to say something but he can't. The figure passes him and disappears.

Suddenly there is a bang. Perele looks up with an angry flicker in her eyes, her little mouth is twisted. "One day she is going to kill herself. We tell her not to crawl around, to stay in one place, but no, she has to behave like a ghost and scare my poor uncle to death. As if he isn't hurt enough already."

Melzer rushes in from his salon with a fearful look on his face. He glances at Perele and sees that her eyes are full of tears. Then he remembers the guest and his face turns red in shame, as if he has been caught in some obscene act. It does not last longer than a second. He runs into the kitchen where he tries to pick up his wife who is lying paralysed on the stone floor. She is as heavy as a corpse. Eventually he leads her back into the room like a small child. He props her up on an old armchair covered with half a dozen shabby cushions, and he pleads with her.

"I beg you, Feygele, don't try to do anything. Everything is being done for you, isn't it? You know that you are weak."

"I am not weak!" The little woman hisses and bites her lips. One can hear in these four words a whole world of protest against her husband, against her niece, against life, against God himself. She is just sitting there as if she were dead. It is hard to know whether she has hurt herself or not. It seems as if she is almost smiling. Yes, indeed, she is smiling. An air of mute happiness surrounds her.

The door of the salon opens and a tall, slender woman walks in. She has an abundance of golden hair and she is dressed in an elegant grey suit. Pinned to the left lapel is a golden monogram, together with a small bunch of fresh flowers. Her low-cut blouse, which is made of blue taffeta silk, shows off real pearls around her wrinkled neck. Her slender, yellowish white hands, with long, red fingernails are laden with diamond rings. She is wearing a ring of dark silver so big that it covers half of her middle finger. Around her wrists are several bracelets, one of which is covered in precious stones. The large brooch crowning her décolleté is full of different animals, birds and dragons, their snouts and wings sprinkled with tiny diamonds.

"Hello, Mr Melzer!" she calls out cheerfully.

"Hello, Madam Zesha, how are you? Did you have a good time?"

"Is it possible to have a good time without you?" she smiles roguishly and winks at him.

The customers are all looking at her. They practically devour her with their eyes. One of them even gives her a light tap when she passes by. She lifts her lovely golden head and walks slowly into the room:

"Oh Perele, my darling, I want a cup of tea! I am simply dying for a cup of tea, and I am hungry too."

Perele goes into the kitchen to fetch tea for the woman who is her aunt on her mother's side.

"Sit down, don't lift a finger!" she says while stretching out both hands to her niece. "I will make myself a cup of tea. You have done enough, my sweetheart. They will suck the strength out of your bones, you little fool!" All the while, she is examining her long nails, and it is obvious she has no intention of making her own tea. Suddenly she notices the guest.

"Oh, I do beg your pardon! I just didn't see you. I am very pleased to meet you," she says, stretching out a long, wrinkled hand, and she then goes into the kitchen to wash her hands. She notices the broken crockery on the polished counter. Some of it is still lying on the stone floor.

"Oy, she's such a pain in the neck! She has scared the wits out of everyone again. She really is too much!" he starts ranting, as if she and not the sick woman were the lady of the house, and she has been terribly embarrassed by the other's behaviour. She comes in again with one hand on her low-necked blouse, and while taking a bite from a piece of cake her eyes wander approvingly over the table, which is covered in delicacies.

"What do you think of my niece?" she asks the guest.

"A fine child, extremely fine."

"Oh, if only you knew. If her mother were still alive. My God! The child was born for the piano, not the sink. The education she was given; the fine schools, and the piano teacher. If only you knew... Her piano teacher was one of the greatest German professors. He said that this child would take the world by storm one day with her talent, and now she has to serve that!" She points her finger at the sick woman. "I ask you, can you tell me why such a thing is alive? She has no children. My sister had to die, but this one here is alive. No children, no eyes, no body, no life! Every once in a while she gives you the creeps! When she falls down, you think to yourself, right, that's it, it's over. But no!"

The short, dark woman is sucking both cheeks inside her mouth. Suddenly she looks gaunt, as if she has holes in her face. She is picking at the flesh of her swollen little hands, and she smiles her dead smile.

After she has finished eating and being coquettish with the guest, Madam Zesha goes upstairs to lie down for a while. In the meantime Perele cooks lunch, which is eaten only in the evening here, and she lays the table. Melzer comes in and throws off his coat. He tidies his hair with a comb, which Perele passes him. Everybody takes a seat at the table.

Melzer sits at the head of the table, with Perele on his right, and Madam Zesha on his left. The guest has been given a seat next to her, and then at the very far end of the table sits the lady of the house.

The sick woman takes a small mirror out of her pocket and tidies her hair. She places both hands on the table like someone who has nothing to do.

"What have you brought with you today, comrade?" Melzer asks the writer.

"I have only recently published one of my best books. Mr Melzer, I can assure you, this time I have surpassed myself. Do you remember my last book? Do you remember the wonderful depictions of people, animals, nature, everything? But still, it wasn't as good as this one. This is an absolute masterpiece, I swear. No Yiddish writer has ever written such an important book. I count on you, Mr Melzer, a long life to you. I know what a fine person you are. And a colleague at that."

"Me? A colleague? I am not a writer, am I?"

"Who is saying that? Of course you are a writer. One can tell from that letter that was published in the local paper that you have great talent. I was simply bowled over by it. So what do you think, would you be able to sell a lot of my books to your customers?"

"I will do everything I can. I am sure I can sell at least a dozen."

The writer gets up, takes a book out of his bag and hands it over to his host. Melzer takes a good look at the subtitle, which takes up a considerable amount of space, and smiles contentedly. He puts his coat back on and is already standing on the doorstep, when he promises that he will write down a list of names of prominent local Jews - and quietly slips a few bank notes into his guest's hand.

In the evening Melzer turns the sign on the glass door saying *Closed* to the street. As it is a summer evening, he takes a chair outside and sits down in front of the door to read a little. He is not able to read for long. Neighbours come from all over the street to have a chat with him. They want to know his opinion on this, that and the other. They are looking deep into his eyes, waiting to hear what he will say. Melzer has an answer for everyone.

Perele and her aunt have gone for a walk. Perele wants to talk to her, but her aunt is doing most of the talking.

"You are a silly little girl, broken shards outlast whole pots. Besides, what do you like about him? He is an old man, after all. I am sure he is in his fifties."

"But aunt, who told you I have such a thing in mind? My uncle loves me as if I were his own child."

"Oh, for heaven's sake, don't make a fool of yourself. I've got eyes in my head - thank God. When one has been married three times, one knows something about these matters! Let him give you some money, then you can leave for America. Your brother there wouldn't make you work like a servant.

You should play the piano, that's what you should do. That is your profession, not cooking."

"But who will look after my uncle?"

"And who will look after you, when you are an old maid?"

"Aunt, I can't allow you to..."

"*Nu*, then I will say it without your permission. And where is the house he was supposed to buy in your name?"

"I don't need a house."

"You don't need it?"

"My God, I am losing my mind," the girl cries out as she is clasping her head with both hands. She trembles, tears glistening through her long black eyelashes. One by one they trickle down her dark cheeks, leaving lines in the powder on her face.

Upon their arrival back home they find Melzer lying asleep with his head on the table. He is resting on a piece of paper, a list with names. His sick wife who sits next to him is stroking him. She looks so soft and sweet, as if she were a baby being fed at her mother's breast.

As soon as the sick woman hears that *"they"* are back, she sneaks out like a thief and goes back to her usual seat in the corner. And all the time she is smiling her endless smile.

"Perele, stay here. Don't walk away, sit down. Yes, you're a good girl!" Madame Zesha says, as she comes downstairs dressed in a sumptuous nightgown, the satin shoulders embroidered with flowers, and a pair of red satin slippers on her feet. As usual, she is clutching an enormous handbag, in which she keeps the entire fortune of her three rich husbands who are all dead.

The writer has also returned. He apologises for having stayed away so long. He tells Melzer that when he does ever manage to sell a book, the purchasers expect him to sit and listen to their life stories. They all assure him that they themselves would have written novels, if only they had the patience.

"*Nu*, well, what can you do? They've no need to ask any questions," the writer sighs deeply and sits down at the table.

"Perele, take a seat, I will make tea," Madam Zesha says, but pulls her own chair a bit closer to the table. So close even that both Melzer and the writer can smell all her perfumes and the different creams she is wearing.

Finally, everyone goes to bed.

Melzer leads his wife into their bedroom. He lies down on his back and stares at the ceiling. Unlike other nights, he is not reading. He is thinking. He tries to recapture something of the dream he had earlier that day during his afternoon nap on the table. His sick wife is lying next to him, the heavy eyelids covering her dull eyes. She does not move. The body simply lies as heavy and cold as a lump of earth. As if she were dead.

Suddenly she hears her husband's voice.

"Are you asleep, Feygele?"

"No, why?" she asks full of surprise, because she has been lying awake next to him all night for years. Awake and silent, while he reads without ever asking her anything. He never utters as much as a word. As if she were merely part of the bed, a piece of wood. And now this!

The woman feels a sudden stir of life inside. This is the first time since the Blitz she has felt like this. It makes her weep. She is crying warm, silent tears. They are streaming down her cheeks: she is like a plant, which has lain dormant for a long time; its roots are deep inside the earth. They still have some life left in them. She is a flower that wilted because of a long drought, but which suddenly feels the first drops of pleasant, warm summer rain. It starts to show signs of life. So warming are the four words he has spoken to her, that they revive her cold, half-dead body. Her breasts, her belly, her knees that always feel frozen, now start to warm up slowly. It is as if her brain itself has become light and clear. She feels young again, and playful, almost mischievous. Yes, mischievous. She remembers love with the man who has become such a distant stranger, albeit so near, who just says "time to go to bed, Feygele", or "don't be foolish", or "don't wander around all the rooms, so people believe that you can actually see", or "don't annoy Perele with your smile." Now he is being as sweet as he used to be years ago. He even turns around to face her. He wipes away her tears and says: "Try to sleep, Feygele."

But she does not sleep. She lies awake, and remembers herself at home with her parents. Her father is cross with her because she is singing. Girls should not sing, according to him. Her mother is shouting at her: "Feygele, walk normally. Why do you dance around as if you are crazy?" They pretend to be angry but deep down they adore her. She once heard her mother say to her father: "Don't worry, we will manage to find a *shidduch*, a match for Feygele even without a dowry. She is a real beauty, may no harm come to her."

At the time it had made her laugh. She knew that she did not need any *shidduch*. She was in love with Berl and she wanted to marry him.

And she looks at the house opposite, the house of the barber-surgeon. There, on the first floor, Berl is standing in his shiny white coat. He is smoking a cigarette and he exhales so skilfully through his nostrils that the smoke spirals upwards, as if by magic. Then he blows the smoke over the balcony in the direction where she is sitting with her little sister in her arms. Her fiery eyes flash a smile back at him. "Black diamonds" - that is what Berl used to call her eyes during their secret meetings. She recalls how her mother would not allow her to stand on the balcony: "What are you standing there for like a *golem*, like a lump of clay? It is not your child, so why be afraid to drop it, right?... The girl is mad as a hatter, she has left the broom in the middle of the room only to sit here and stare at nothing...get inside, do you hear me?"

She remembers how Berl once sent her a little note through the apprentice boy. Her mother, who was bending over the cradle in the alcove to feed the baby, came running to the door, but in her haste she had forgotten to button up her blouse. One of her breasts was just hanging there, naked. She just about managed to see the boy off. Feygele laughed so hard. Oh, how funny her mother looked that day. And the boy had whistled all the way downstairs.

"What did he want? Tell me!" her mother shouted at her.

"He wanted to know when the afternoon prayers start today. It is the anniversary of the death of the barber-surgeon."

"Oh really? You see, there is nothing stronger than a Jewish soul," her mother said, and walked back to the child that was screaming for attention. Feygele can still hear her screaming.

She thinks about Perele, how she took her out of Germany. Feygele wanted to be a mother and a father to her. And now she is thinking about her brother. He used to play tricks on her whenever he could, just like her father. And now there is his daughter. "She thinks that I don't know what she is up to. From the moment she arrived here she has put me to one side, telling me that I am blind. She has taken over everything. They have even convinced the doctor that I am blind. I can see well enough to watch my enemies' downfall. I can see things now, and there is not that much light. How can I be blind?" Suddenly she turns around to face her husband and she touches his shoulder.

Melzer sits up immediately. He thinks his wife is ill.

"Hah? What's the matter?" he says while rubbing his eyes.

"Nothing. Nothing at all. But I wanted to ask you what it was you were talking about this afternoon in your sleep. You kept saying 'Feygele', 'Perele', 'Feygele', 'Perele'. What were you dreaming about?"

"I wasn't dreaming about anything. I wasn't dreaming at all," Melzer says half with anger, half with kindness. He turns over.

She is beyond tears. She feels how her body is filling up with lead again, how it becomes heavy, dead almost. She is lying there next to her husband like a piece of risen dough. He is sleeping peacefully. She is only able to fall asleep just before the dawn.

On the Sabbath, Melzer invites the writer to his place. After the meal, Madam Zesha and Perele make themselves smart. In the meantime, Melzer takes a nap at the table and afterwards he helps his wife get into her Sabbath clothes. The sick woman powders her face blindly, and some of it falls on her black coat and on her shoes. She checks her appearance in a little mirror. They set out on a bus tour in honour of their guest.

The bus sways and jolts along and finally they end up somewhere south of the city. There the fields are vast and green, cut into symmetrical lines. On both sides of the fields there are rows of little white houses with red tiles on the roof and delightful little front gardens. There is music and sunshine everywhere. Girls and boys are playing tennis on a patch of grass, and every time the ball rolls out of sight, they burst into laughter. Youngsters are galloping by on horseback. They are all wearing fine costumes and brightly shining boots. If it were not for the occasional sight of neatly coiffed hair on a feminine shoulder, it would be impossible to tell the boys from the girls.

"Why don't you buy a house here? You work hard the whole week. You could really relax here during the weekends, and even on weekday evenings," the writer observes. Melzer sighs: "Because my wife doesn't want it."

"She doesn't want it? But it would help her illness too."

"*Nu*, you can see for yourself, can't you? She wants to be with me day and night. She is afraid of being alone. She feels good there amongst the ruins, she says."

"Alone? But why can't she stay with your niece? She's a good girl. A kind girl. And Madam Zesha, she's cheerful, no?"

"She is about to go away. She has only been here for a couple of months. And my niece shouldn't live alone with my wife. It's not right to condemn a young girl to a life with a sick person."

"It's a shame," the writer sighs. "If you had a house here, you could organise a literary evening for me here."

"I would do it with pleasure."

The bus comes to a halt. Madam Zesha takes the writer by the arm. Perele walks on the other side of him. They are happily chattering away, all three of them, and they quickly forget about Melzer, who has to lead his small, heavy wife.

She walks with little, stumbling steps, like a child that is learning to walk. It is tiring for him to try and move so slowly. He forces himself to walk with the same small steps, but nevertheless he is going too fast. It is suffocating for him. He feels hot and heavy. He starts to sweat, and he wipes his forehead constantly. He feels envious of the three people in front of him who can walk as freely and as quickly as they want. His wife, nearly blind and paralysed, leans heavily on his tired arm. She drags him down with her towards the ground.

# *Clocks*

Mrs Jacobson stood there again that evening, just as she always did. She was all ready to go out, with a brown suitcase in one hand, and a blue and white striped woollen blanket in the other. She was pleading with her daughter, who was about twenty years old, with a small, turned-up nose and bright, amber-coloured eyes - intelligent, smiling eyes - to come along and spend the night in the shelter:

"Come with me. Stop torturing me like this. Long live Hitler! You're such a stubborn girl! It will be a miracle if I get a night's sleep. Why do you have to be so obstinate?"

"Mother, I'm not going to drag myself in and out of shelters as long as I have a *room* and a bed to sleep in. I have told you a thousand times already. "*Goodnight*, mother and *good luck!*"

Mrs Jacobson bit her lip and went out, mumbling a prayer to God, may He protect her child, her bad child, and may He forgive her for causing her mother such heartache.

"She's such a silly girl! She doesn't understand!" She tried to explain to the Almighty that her daughter Bella was a good girl deep down, and that He should protect her and make sure that no harm came to her. She walked out through the garden gate lost in thought.

The small front garden was ablaze with colours and bursting with birdsong. The bright flowers of late summer were talking to each other intimately in their own, wordless language. They stood there idly, bathed in the golden light of the setting sun, no longer of use to any living creature. Nobody looked at them or smelled their wonderful fragrance. The small trees, which had once been pruned, and tamed by metal wire, now grew wild, and they wondered why nobody took care of them anymore. Not even Bella.

The alleyway exuded an air of Yom Kippur - beautiful, sad and eerily quiet.

Mrs Jacobson shuffled along the empty pavement with her luggage in both hands, sighing wearily.

A neighbour rushed past her like a whirlwind, shouting over his shoulder *"All the best!"* and before she knew it, he had disappeared. He was running to secure a place in an underground station, otherwise he might end up having to spend the whole night standing up.

Mrs Jacobson, deep in thought, did not answer him straightaway. When she realised what had happened, she started running after him. Just as on Yom Kippur she could not afford to offend anyone.

*"All the best!"* she called out desperately, in the silence of the evening.

Bella was lying in her narrow, child's bed. She listened to the roaring Nazi aeroplanes and to the dull, faraway explosions and gunfire, which became increasingly clear as the planes came nearer. She heard the whistling sound of the bombs, which by now were coming down almost onto her own roof. As they fell, some of them wept like little children, others howled like mad dogs. She could see the flames through the window, rising up to the sky. Then another fire exploded in the blazing sky with such force it was as if somebody had poured a barrel of petrol onto a burning building. It lit up her girlish bedroom and the bed she was lying in. A strange feeling of excitement took hold of her. She pulled the silk blanket closer to her face, and watched the spectacle with both fear and curiosity. She even fell asleep for a moment. When she woke up again, she was surprised at herself: "Hmm...oh dear...to fall asleep at a moment like this!"

It was almost morning when the sirens finally sounded the *all clear*. There was nothing she wanted more than to turn around and sleep for half a day, but the office was waiting. So she got up about an hour and a half later, and exactly at the same time as every other day, at eight o'clock precisely, she was already half dressed downstairs in the *morning room*. As usual, she first gave the cat a bowl of milk. Then she put the kettle on, and started doing her exercises.

"One! Two! Feet together! Don't bend the knees! Hands on your hips!

One! Two!" the lady on the radio called out energetically. Music followed. The kettle hummed cheerfully on the gas stove.

Bella spluttered as she threw cold water onto her face. She quickly brushed her amber hair. She was still finishing her *cup of tea*, as she walked to the door, wearing her coat and carrying a small handbag.

"Are you off already?"

She saw her mother, dressed in what seemed to be a dozen coats and carrying her luggage with both hands.

"A fine night we've had. Hitler should be so lucky! God forbid, I didn't sleep a wink! But who cares?"

Bella smiled.

"*Goodbye*, mother, it's late," she said, and she stretched out her small, pale hand with the long, red fingernails to check the time. Bella wanted to give her mother a kiss, but all she could see of her mother's face were two bloodshot eyes. The rest was wrapped up. So she planted a kiss on the blue, woollen scarf which she had knitted for her mother so that she could protect herself against the draughts down in the underground, and left the house.

The front garden was veiled in bright, silver sunlight that morning. The flowers warmed themselves in the sunshine and the last drops of dew were disappearing rapidly. Bella picked a flower and put it in her lapel. A small drop quivered on one of the leaves for a second, and then vanished.

Together with the flower, Bella had picked up a pointed piece of grey metal. It had sharp edges and was still warm. She put it away in her elegant handbag, so that she could show it to her colleagues at the office.

"It will be a souvenir," she thought, and hurried to the bus stop.

The earth lay there like a corpse prepared for an autopsy, its innards wet and glistening. Sewage pipes were sticking out everywhere, like intestines falling out of an open belly.

The trolley bus had to wind its way through endless side streets because all the main roads had been closed off and lined with signs saying Danger! No Through Traffic! Finally, Bella reached her destination.

"Good morning! Do you recognise the place where our building used to be?" Her boss greeted her with a broad smile. He rubbed his hands contentedly and his face beamed with happiness.

"It happened five minutes after I left. I had been staying late, last night, to sort out some bills. God has been very good to me! Do you know how many people got killed here?"

Bella looked up. Suddenly she started shaking so violently that her boss only just managed to keep her on her feet, helping her with his big, strong hands.

And there it was, in the ruined street, among the piles of bricks, earth, bent metal joists and glass, and the smoke and smouldering fires which the firemen had not yet managed to extinguish: the high-pitched, regular ticking of their office clock. It was still hanging on the one remaining wall, which was covered in black smoke. It ticked monotonously, vibrating slightly, like the only soul left living in a cemetery.

"Tick-tock! Tick-tock!"

Bella looked again at the dark wall. There was such horror in her eyes when she stared at the clock, that it frightened her boss. On the way home, the melancholy, drawn-out wail of the sirens sounded again.

The bus stopped. Bella had not intended to go into any shelter, but suddenly, without knowing how she got there, she found herself in the basement of a church, together with the other passengers from the bus.

Gloomy old women sat on low benches, boxes and stones, with quivering, toothless mouths, their dead eyes smiling in a mechanical fashion. They were busy knitting socks and gloves for the *boys* with their thin, black-veined hands.

The air downstairs in the cellar was grey and foggy. It smelled of mould and the chill of graves.

*Wardens* dressed in blue aprons with silver buttons helped the older children down the stairs. All the children were crying. The emergency lights which gave out a dark and cheerless glow, spread more shadow than light. The women just kept on knitting.

"Why are you looking at me like that?" one of the women asked Bella.

Her voice startled Bella; she thought that the clock had suddenly started talking to her. She began swaying with such force that the old lady could barely prevent her from falling down.

"Sit down," she panted heavily, and offered Bella a seat next to her on a gravestone.

Bella looked around. Only then did she realise that the place was full of gravestones: some were large and impressive, others low and humble; there were smooth stones and carved ones; there were really tiny stones on children's graves, and old, green stones covered in moss. She shivered. It seemed to her as if these women, with their yellow, crumpled faces and sad smiles in their lacklustre eyes, their toothless mouths trembling constantly, were in fact the corpses who had come out of their graves, and who were now sitting on their own gravestones, quietly knitting socks and gloves for death itself. She started to make her way towards the door.

"What are you afraid of?" The old woman kept on talking to Bella. "You are in the right place. If anything happens, you don't even need to have a funeral," she joked. "We sit here all night long, and often part of the day as well," she babbled on. "The air is not good in here, but at least it's safer than outside." The old woman spoke reassuringly, as she made herself comfortable again on the gravestone. Her dull eyes still smiled their dead smile.

Bella came out onto the street. Outside one could hear the explosions and the muted gunfire. She breathed freely, eagerly drawing the fresh, cool air into her lungs. She walked home.

The front garden was brimming with life again. The golden light of the afternoon flowed freely; the flowers looked magnificent. She opened the door. The house had never been so dear to her as at that moment.

Suddenly she noticed the clock on the mantelpiece. Their homely, old clock. Her mother, luggage in hand, stood next to it. She was ready to go to the shelter, even earlier than usual.

"Wait, mother, I'm coming with you. Wait, wait, wait! I'm afraid of...of the clocks." Bella did not see one clock, but hundreds of them all around her. They stood there, not on the mantelpiece, where a bright fire was spreading an intimate feeling of warmth and cosiness, but on gravestones. The gravestones were old and green, overgrown with moss, and they were saying something to each other, mumbling in their own secret language.

"Wait, mother, wait! Wait!"

Mrs Jacobson, her bloodshot eyes wide open, did not understand what her daughter was saying. But she quietly praised the Almighty for giving her daughter the wisdom, at last, to see that it was better to go and sleep in the shelter...after all.

# *Blitz*

A drawn-out wail, heavy and melancholy. The announcement coming from the siren sounded like a song of lamentation.

The people living round the docks did not even have enough time to be frightened.

"It came down suddenly. It seemed to fall straight from heaven," the East Enders would say afterwards.

The heavens had expanded over the city, as wide and clear as if they were hovering somewhere over the Orient, and not over wet, misty London, bathing eternally in soot, smoke, and darkness. Its inhabitants were pale and withdrawn, haunted by the dampness that pervaded everything.

It was September and the sun poured its cruel heat over the black city, covering the grime that had been gathering for years, in the little alleyways, on the identical, flat-faced houses.

The rays of the sun were fierce and penetrating. They crept into the wrinkles of poor people's skin, revealing the dark pores, the tiniest hairs on a chin or mole, and the blue lips of old and middle-aged Gentile women, who had just come outside with their baskets and purses, their wages fresh in their hands, ready to go and buy meat for the Sunday roast.

It was the afternoon of the Jewish Sabbath. The Gentile women, and those Jewish women who worked on Saturdays, were all in a hurry. They were on their hands and knees, busy scrubbing lime onto the doorsteps of the narrow house entrances. Copper doorknockers were being polished until they shone as brilliantly as the sun whose rays were caught in them.

Canaries could be seen hopping around in their cages in low, broad windows with chequered wooden panes. These had lost their wooden appearance a long time ago and now looked more like old, corroded tin, peeling and crumbling everywhere.

Satisfied, filled with the warmth of the bright sun, the birds were singing cheerfully, oblivious of the war taking over the world.

Cats were sitting nearby, looking with wondering eyes at the frenzied cleaning, as if they were about to ask the women what the point was of washing doorsteps and polishing knockers at a time of war, when there were so many more urgent things to be done.

The Jewish women who had already rested were sitting outside the small houses. They discussed the war: the sons who were in the army, and those who would be called up soon to help to protect England, and to save the world from that crazy brute.

Mothers sighed and assured each other that with God's help he would die a violent death, that Hitler.

The men were in shirtsleeves because of the heat. They sat rocking on low kitchen stools while telling their neighbours it was a sin to talk like that: "The more one swears at him, the stronger he gets!" - adding curses of their own. "May he die in torment!"

"So what? Heaven and earth have sworn that the world will not come to an end," the old Bible scholar Abrams threw in, as he closed his copy of the *Eyn Yankev*.

And tall Simon, a Jewish boxer, made a fist. "We will show him," he said, and he squeezed his hand so tightly that you saw his five white knuckles, which looked as if they could kill a man with one blow.

"Of course not. The world will not come to an end," Jews comforted themselves, and the sun melted the creases on their Sabbath faces into a smile. Its light crept inside the narrowest of houses, through half-open doors of homes that looked like black crates.

"A wonderful world, if only we were allowed to enjoy it," the mothers said as they tried to wipe away stubborn tears, which reappeared as soon as they had dried up.

Little girls raced past them on the cobblestones, small whirlwinds of silk and satin, jumping over ropes, flaunting flowing locks of hair. Their mothers had tried to outdo each other, skilfully creating snake-like curls.

The sun made its way into every little corner. It slid down behind a clothes hanger, and onto the peeling furniture in a house basking in its Sabbath mood. In a shop, the light crept over a few green apples, a shrivelled bunch of parsley, a couple of wrinkled tomatoes, and a head of garlic. Carefully it threaded the blue lines of a silk *tallis*, weaving itself into the prayer shawl's string of tassels. It warmed and lit up the gold leaf on all kinds of holy books and women's prayer books in a neighbourhood bookstore. Then it disappeared discreetly into the background, so as not to trouble the gramophone records, *Brivele der Mamen* and *Rozhinkes mit Mandlen*, and the Haggodahs for Pesach, which had all been cleared away out of respect for the approaching High Holidays, and which were now lying peacefully under a layer of dust.

Boys and girls were getting ready to go out and leave the hot, narrow streets, which smelt of rotting fruit, scorched trousers - from being in the tailors' workshops - horse dung and stables. They had their minds set on a part of London where the streets were not all tangled up and cut off by the Commercial Road. They were longing for a part of the city where the streets were broad, beautiful and spacious. Even in these days, the windows were covered with brown strips of paper all the time, and grey sandbags were piled up around magnificent buildings, hiding half of the display windows.

Youngsters looked as neat as a new pin. Girls combed their hair until it was shining and smooth; their fingernails polished to perfection. The boys seemed to have been bathing themselves in brilliantine. The creases in their trousers were as sharp as knives. None of them seemed troubled by the fact that soon they would be leaving for the front. Quite the reverse; they would rather go today than tomorrow!

"Oy, how we will hit them!" The young men could hardly wait to give the enemy a hell of a time. Their Jewish hearts were burning with the desire to beat the Nazis. But, in the meantime, until they would be called up, life was there to be lived.

"Oy-oy-oooooy," wails the siren, imploring the young not to go. It is dangerous and even before its sound has died away, one can hear explosions, together with the roar of hundreds of aeroplanes. They are like birds of prey, filling the sky with their flashing steel. "Bang-boom!" and the little black houses are blown in all directions, like shards of coal under a miner's hammer. Suffocating black smoke is carried this way from burning buildings in the docks.

Long rows of houses are on fire in no time at all. Flames dance in a pandemonium behind every window. They stick out fiery, licking tongues and look like devils - strangely beautiful, even. The flames come in many different shades of green, red, yellow, orange - a feast of colour, as if to make fun of humanity and signify its ruin. The food supplies for the coming winter are all on fire. The food had been brought over by brave seamen. They risked their lives to take care of this country, which has not provided for itself with ripe cornfields, nor with its own bread, like other nations have done.

The barges lie burning on the Thames, like low mountains on fire. It seems as if the river itself will soon be on fire. The Thames and the sky: both seas of blood.

In the alleyways, men and women flee in all directions, dragging with them their own and other people's children. Some of the children are crying, others are struck dumb with terror. They try to save themselves, but they cannot find a way out. Death is lurking everywhere. Glass is falling, it is raining bricks, the roofs come crashing down, whole houses are collapsing - all at once. Human beings are buried alive; men, women and children.

Their cries and the groans of the wounded are drowned out by the shouts of people standing outside their front doors who do not want to leave their ruined homes. Recklessly, they grapple with the fire, wanting to remove the debris with their bare hands, the molten lumps of earth and the bent iron beams glowing from the heat. In an attempt to drag out the people who are still alive, they only succeed in burying themselves.

The lamenting around the ruins becomes increasingly bitter, when people find the bodies of their own mothers and fathers, their own children and neighbours.

"Where is God?" asks the wife of old Abrams and she looks up at the brightly lit sky.

But a bomb blast hurls her away. She lies there motionless, clutching her wig tightly in one hand. She does not ask any more questions.

Tall Simon has been working tirelessly. He has pulled body after body out from under the rubble, handing them over to the emergency workers. Crippled bodies, covered in blood, some of them dead. Now, all of a sudden, he loses his mind. The relentless neighing of the horses in their locked-up stables in the docklands is too much for him. He abandons everything, and walks away, treading on the living and the dead.

Then, he throws himself into the fire and rips open the stable doors. A numb panic surrounds the horses as they leap out.

They gallop wildly off into the narrow streets, trampling everything underfoot. Within seconds, they are like running torches, fleeing the suffocating smoke. They collapse in mid-flight, stretching out as if in silent protest, with their hooves raised to the blazing sky.

Night was falling. The sun was going down, enflamed and glowing red. The heavens were left to bleed. Two fires lit up the sky: one in the east and one in the west.

The Nazi aeroplanes were still there. Just like the spiders who once brought fire to the Temple, they flew in more and more bombs to drop on the Jewish alleyways, where nothing was left to destroy.

# Dogs

Tom turned the few coins between his bony fingers and stared at them with hard, grey eyes. He had no idea what to do next. He had only one thought in his head. His conscience was troubling him. He knew perfectly well that what his wife said was true - he never had any luck with the dogs. He had already pawned his winter coat, as well as the linen. All that was left were a couple of swaddling clothes for the baby. He had not paid the rent for the last three weeks. The landlord had given him notice that day, warning that if he did not pay up, he would be thrown out on the street, together with his wife and child, even though it was the middle of winter.

"Do as I say. Don't go! You'll see, you will lose again! My heart's heavy and I know what that means. You know my heart can always tell what's going to happen! Every time I tell you not to go, you lose!" Mrs Dickson said as she studied her husband's steely expression to see if he was listening to a word that she said. She stood next to a rusty tin tub rubbing the baby's clothes between her thin fingers. The washing stayed dirty because there had been no money to buy soap.

"Do what I say. Take him this week's money and tell him that we'll pay the rest off, one shilling a week. He'll say yes, I know he will."

Tom did not answer her. He saw how the child was gnawing a crust of bread. The saliva was running out of his little mouth. He had started biting the big toe on his left foot from sheer hunger. His face was pale, the small eyes were red and swollen. The foot pointing up in the air looked green, bony and crooked.

He became angry with the infant.

"Stop biting your toe," he snapped, while hastily pulling it out of the baby's mouth. Now he started crying; teardrops were running down the wan cheeks and into his little blue mouth.

Tom got even angrier.

He stood up. He looked through the dirty windowpanes and saw the big clock above the public house, the White Elephant. It was already very late.

"Come along if you want to. It won't make any difference now. This time I'm going to win - you'll see. Listen, I'm going to go anyway. If you come with me, it'll cost one shilling more, but that way you'll see the result there and then. You'll save yourself from lying here miserable, all alone. Come on, it'll do you good!"

He had already brought out her faded coat. It had once been brown. She would not know what colour to call it now. She was ashamed to wear it, even to go to the dogs. The child was dressed in old rags that had become too small, and Tom no longer had an overcoat.

But what was she going to do otherwise on such a long, dreary evening? Besides - if he won and she was not with him - he might end up in the White Elephant to celebrate his winnings with his mates and then she would still be left with nothing.

She combed her thin hair, wrapped up the baby and set out to try her luck.

"Those people are all crazy! They would give their lives for the dogs. Just look at what is going on there!" Mrs Dickson marvelled, as if she was witnessing the spectacle for the very first time.

Tom had forgotten the cold. He did not feel the water coming in through the holes in his shoes, soaking his feet. He had bought two tickets and he radiated happiness.

"I have placed our bet on Black Albert, he's a sure thing! I know we'll be lucky today."

"I doubt it," Mrs Dickson thought to herself. She sighed. Nevertheless, she was drawn into what was happening around her.

Her heart was beating fast. What was she going to do if he lost again?

"He won't," she thought resolutely, pushing away her gloomy thoughts. Now that she was here she would pray to God and beg Him to send them the winner. For once, only today. "No, no, no! He can't lose. He won't lose today. Of course he'll win." She was trying to fend off the terrible thoughts, which were forcing themselves on her.

She looked around. The crowd was getting more and more excited. They only had one thought in their heads - the dogs. Twenty thousand people had come there to watch this canine spectacle.

Electric lamps throw a dim, dark shine on a round patch of grass cut very short, creating the illusion of a green lake. A circular strip of grass runs around the "water". It is ablaze with light. On it stands a white, freshly painted pen, which looks like a doll's house from a distance.

The arena is beautiful.

People with money are seated comfortably on a separate balcony, similar to boxes in a theatre. The whole place is lit in a festive manner. The lights are twinkling. Dozens of lamps are dazzling people's eyes. A large building resembling a factory is taking in flashy cars and the rich punters. The darkness outside absorbs the buses, which have taken the poor to the dog track as if guided by their blood and tears.

The "water" and the strip of grass around it creates a division between the rich visitors and the rest. On one side an entry ticket costs five shillings, on the other only one.

The one-shillingers are pouring in from all over London. The buses that are pulling up are packed with human flesh, with human sweat and human folly. And it is not only the buses, but trolley cars as well that are bursting with people. London is going to the dogs!

Red-faced bookies keep close to their stands, trading happiness for just a few shillings, offering red sheets of paper with the names of all the dogs.

The crowds descend on them like bees on honey.

The bookies are raving, their faces growing ever redder. Their eagerness to attract ever more customers gives them strength.

Their loud cries can be heard everywhere.

"Two to one, four to one!"

There is the blare of trumpets. The masses stop swarming around like insects. Some people sit down, others remain standing. All eyes are focused on the arena. All hearts are pounding with anticipation.

Six men dressed in white coats, like doctors, are leading out six slender, good-looking dogs. They are wearing little jackets so that they will not catch colds, God forbid! They are paraded around the stadium. The dogs have a haughty bearing; they do not deign to look at their mostly dishevelled fans, many of whom are wearing torn trousers. Few have overcoats. They shiver with cold.

The dogs are led into the pen. A stuffed, white hare is brought out onto the circular strip of grass. The hare runs on electricity. You can hear a racket from inside the pen. The dogs are howling with excitement. Their barking gets mixed in with the buzz of the tense crowd. Suddenly the lights go out. Silence.

The door from the pen is lifted. The hare shoots out - followed by the half-crazed dogs.

The crowd goes wild with excitement. People are screaming at the top of their voices.

"Go on, Mick! Good old Mick! Go on! Beat them!"

"Go on Black Albert! Run! Show them! Go on! Go on! Go on!"

The hare disappears. One dog has reached the finish. Dead silence. Disappointed faces. Downcast expressions. Only a few people are walking up the stairs. They approach the bookies to claim their winnings, their faces glowing. The others stay exactly where they are. They look like losers.

The bookies look satisfied. They go about their business with renewed energy. Tom feels in his pockets.

He decides to try one more time. He has to try to win back all the money he's lost. The bookies have their hands full.

Smartly turned-out gentlemen, stiff hats on their greased heads and spotless white gloves on their kosher hands, signal to the other side who has won.

After just fifteen minutes fresh dogs are brought in. The whole ritual is repeated seven or eight times more, and then the last race is over.

The crowd disperses. Mrs Dickson, the child in her arms, the colour drained from her face, is crying bitterly.

"How am I going to buy milk for the baby? How are we going to pay the rent this week?" she snivels. Tom's eyes are bloodshot. He is shivering in his thin jacket. His hands are deep inside his pockets. He gives his wife threatening looks, warning her to keep quiet, not to make things worse with her moaning.

Young Jewish men who only yesterday were reading prayer books and who today are petit bourgeois, wealthy women who belong to all kinds of clubs and societies, had all come to try their luck. And so had the *goyim*, rich, drunk or in a festive mood. They had all come to the dogs.

"*They* will not be thrown out of their homes," Mrs Dickson groans.

"Shut up, I said!" Tom's eyes have a murderous glow. The bustle remains undiminished and it is even worse outside. Little boys dart about in the streets, delivering their news about the triumph of some dog or other.

"All the winners! Read all about it!" The words resound all over London. The newspapers are selling like hot cakes. In the general commotion nobody notices her quiet moaning. Tom has nothing to be afraid of anymore.

*Afterword*

# My Uncle Yitzhak: A Memoir of Isaac Bashevis Singer

## by Maurice Carr

Maurice Carr, the son of Esther Kreitman, was an accomplished writer, editor and journalist in his own right. He was largely responsible for her work becoming known outside the Yiddish-speaking world. He translated her novel *Der Sheydim-tants* (*The Demons' Dance*), which was published in England and America with the title *Deborah*. He also translated some of the stories of her brothers Isaac Bashevis Singer and Israel Joshua Singer (whom he refers to here by his Hebrew name, Shiya). After seeing a newspaper head-line in Paris announcing the death of his uncle Yitzhak, Isaac Bashevis Singer he wrote this vivid piece which gives a tantalising glimpse into the lives of Yiddish's leading literary family.

No matter how estranged and detached they were from the religious beliefs of their forebears and distant from each other, they took their inspira-tion from *Yiddishkayt* - all things Jewish and Yiddish - from family relation-ships and human. This was the stuff of all their work, the glue that bound them together for all time. Carr shows how his mother, "Hindele" as he affec-tionately calls her here, was always in the shadow of her famous brothers, but he was a passionate believer in her and her work. With 2004 being the cente-nary of Isaac Bashevis Singer's birth as well as marking fifty years since Esther Kreitman's death, somehow one feels they would all have enjoyed the irony of their lives still intertwined in a book. The following memoir is a fit-ting epitaph for them all.

"Such," says my uncle Yitzhak, taking an awestruck sniff at his boiled egg, which stinks, "yes, such is life!"

There is a moment of silence, followed by a burst of hilarity that rocks the breakfast table. Yitzhak sits with bowed head over the bad egg, and his air of otherworldly absence raises the merriment to a new pitch. Even his melancholy elder brother Shiya (short for Yehoshua) grins. Shiya's dumpy wife very nearly falls off her chair. Only half-amused is Hindele, sister to the two Singer brothers. With a wry smile she repeats: "Such, yes, such is life!"

Antoshu, the maid, serves a fresh hard-boiled egg, the meal is resumed in a more subdued mood, and little Yossele trills: "When I'm big, I'll take papa up on the roof and give him a whipping!" At two-and-a-half he is bitterly jealous of his father Shiya's favourite, seven-year-old Yasha.

Much has happened since that day on the veranda of a bungalow in a pinewood dacha near Warsaw. Its landlord, the folk poet Alter Katzisner, and the Yiddish literati to whom he rented out a score of such bungalows for the summer, are long since dead. Most, but not all, perished in the Holocaust. The child Yasha died a natural death, of pneumonia, in Warsaw. His father Shiya went down with a heart attack at an early age in New York, and his mother Genya followed. So did Hindele - my mother - some years later, in London, where my parents had come as World War I refugees and where I grew up. The sole survivors are Yossele who has grown up into Joseph Singer living in America, and my own aged Tel Aviv self.

And now it is my uncle Yitzhak's turn. Of all things, it is that buffoonery of his, in the long-ago year of 1926, which comes back to me as I stand before a kiosk in Paris in 1991, staring and stared at by front-page obituaries in the French morning papers for Isaac Bashevis Singer. The leftist daily *Liberation* carries a photograph of him covering two-thirds of the front page. The caption in a large red box announces: "YIDDISH LOSES SINGER. Isaac Bashevis Singer, the last great writer in the Yiddish language, died Wednesday, aged 87. See page 2." I see page 2 and go on to pages 3, 4 and 5, wholly and reverentially devoted to the Nobel laureate of literature, the Singer who sang the swan song of our *mameh loshn*, the Yiddish mother tongue.

I turn again to the front-page photo, a studio portrait of Bashevis - Yiddishists call him simply that - in the pose of a comedian. Against a backdrop of phantoms painted on a screen, he stands holding an umbrella in his outstretched right hand, too far out of line to keep the make-believe rain from his skin-and-bones figure, and wearing sunglasses against the make-believe sunlight. Shabby in an ill-fitting, outsized, expensive suit, with a trilby hat jammed tight on his cranium, he looks tense, though his gaunt face bears a faint smile blending mockery with resignation - the same blend that sets the tone of his masterly novels and short stories.

What do I have to tell that his painstaking biographers and his obituarists in the world media have missed? Well, of utmost relevance to him, who was through no fault of his own my uncle, is the old Yiddish saw: *Dos eppele falt nisht veit fun boimele* (the apple doesn't fall far from the tree), meaning that the key to personality is in the family genes.

The paradoxical was the norm for my uncle Yitzhak. So he, who insisted he did not give two straws for kinship, adopted the pseudonym Bashevis after his mother Bathsheve; to get to know him better, we must first be introduced to her. Quite exceptional, too, was the relationship between him and his elder brother Shiya, known to the world as the novelist I J (for Israel Joshua) Singer.

Long before I, at age thirteen, met my uncle Yitzhak and my grandmother Bathsheve in the flesh - not that there was much flesh on them to speak of - I was on more intimate terms with them than with my next-door cockney neighbours in London. How come? Because from as far back as I can remember, day in, day out, year after year, my mother had plied me in a nostalgic sing-song with reminiscences, detailed and vivid, about her folks in the old country, *die alte heim*.

Where to begin if not at the beginning?

In the latter half of the nineteenth century the small Polish town of Bilgoray boasts an orphan of unknown parentage who is an *ilui*, a genius. He memorises Scripture at a single reading, and mounts the pulpit to deliver his first homily as a boy of nine. At the first sprouting of a beard, the local Hasidim importune him to become their *tzaddik*, their holy man who will hasten the advent of the Messiah and the resurrection of all past generations. But Reb Mordechai, as he is called, declares himself a *misnaged*, a rejecter of end-of-days fantasies and a firm believer in the Torah's rule that mortal man is fated to return eternally to the dust out of which he was created.

Appointed rabbi of Bilgoray, Reb Mordechai is offered positions in

Warsaw and other large cities, but always turns them down. To the delegations who come to petition him he puts a stock question: "Is there a Jewish cemetery in your parts?" Reassured on this score, he turns them away with a shrug: "We also have one in Bilgoray." There is to this *misnaged* rabbi an aura so palpable that he is said to have averted a pogrom one Easter Sunday when, standing in the doorway of the synagogue, with upraised hands he stopped a mob of peasants armed with hatchets and pitchforks. Come to avenge the crucifixion of Jesus, they wavered, backed away, and dispersed without bloodshed and without pillage.

Like father, like daughter. Like Reb Mordechai, so also Bathsheve. She, too, is a genius, and an expert into the bargain in scholarly disputation (*pilpul*), able to hold her own in discourse with the rabbi and to reconcile seemingly blatant contradictions in Torah and Talmud. The rabbi is less fortunate with his two sons. Both are scholars and ordained rabbis, but the one harbours grandiose mercantile dreams, while the other is a dandy whose earlocks and ritual fringes bob, positively waltz, with superb elegance.

Comes puberty and the time for marriage of the near-skeletal maiden with the shock of red hair that will be shaved to accommodate a wig, and with enormous steely eyes in a tiny, fiercely angular, deathly pale face perched proudly on a scrawny neck. The search is on for an intended who will be worthy of her. The choice falls on the teenaged Pinhas Menahem Singer, a Talmudist and kabbalist of the first order, who traces his ancestry back to the medieval sage Joseph Caro and even farther back to David the psalmist king.

If ever a mismatch could be called perfect, this is it. Bathsheve carries in her womanly frame a manly spirit. Unlike her husband, she has in her the makings of a chief rabbi, one who would not have hesitated to accept a pulpit in Warsaw or might even perhaps have betaken herself to Jerusalem. The better to express her grievance against Jehovah, the bungling Maker of her misbirth, she is all the more meticulous in her observance of His divine commandments.

Mysterious are the ways of the Lord. What better husband could Bathsheve have found than Pinhas Menahem, harbouring in his frail but masculine frame a tender, womanly spirit? With a heart as soft and as golden as his fluffy beard, his she-he persona has nothing in it of the warrior monarch. More's the pity that in one respect he does bear a likeness to his royal forefather, the psalmist. As a kind of truant Hasid, he often steals away to the court of the Gerer *tzaddik*, there to dance and sing to the glory of the unutterable Name for weeks on end. To boot, he shirks the Russian-language examination required of the clergy under tsarist law, so that when the time comes for him to act the breadwinner and paterfamilias, he can do no better than serve as a poor clandestine rabbi, first in the poorest of poor *shtetlach*, and later in the slummiest of Warsaw's slums, on Krochmalna Street. All this will be so much grist for the mill of the eventual Singer storyteller.

While the newlyweds are still *kestkinder*, boarders living on the largesse of the Bilgoray rabbi's household, Bathsheve suffers several dread years of sterility. At last, blessedly pregnant, she expects a son - her due, to make amends for her own mistaken gender - but Jehovah sees fit to curse her with a daughter to whom she refuses the breast. The search for a wet nurse yields one whose nipples squirt milk so abundantly that it dribbles all over the face of the unwanted newborn. The infant, named Hinde Esther, is taken away by the wet nurse to a tumbledown one-room shack crammed with a horde of children and a husband pounding away at his cobbler's bench, a shack so crowded that the only floor space for the crib is under the table.

Punctually once a week Bathsheve comes by to stoop and regard, but never to touch, let alone fondle, her misbegotten child - my mother-to-be. At the age of three, blinded by cobwebs and dust from the underside of the table, Hindele is brought home and, with the benediction of the Bilgoray rabbi, she partially recovers her sight. But for the rest of her life her eyelids will either twitch, as if to be rid of the glaze filming her bloodshot eyeballs, or flutter wildly, as if beholding an apparition visible to none but herself.

I learn early on to listen and not to interrupt my mother Hindele's recital of bygones, addressed first and last to herself. Even so, she never fails to answer my unasked questions. Does she remember her under-the-table outcast self and also the happenings and mishaps that took place before ever she was born? Oh, no, she is merely retelling what she heard later from her mother Bathsheva. Storytelling runs in the family.

Oddly enough, my mother is less profuse with her own memories, except for an occasional trance-like recall of her encounters with a handsome, noble, emancipated, clean-shaven young Jewish poet wearing a cloak in

Warsaw's elegant Saxony Gardens. For the rest, she speaks less of herself than of her three brothers - of Shiya, two years younger than herself, with passion, fierce love, and fierce jealousy; of Yitzhak *der roiter*, the redhead, the spitting image of his mother Bathsheve, with amusement; and last but not least, of the toddler Moshe, the golden-haired beauty whose name I, too, bear.

My mother does breathe fire, though, on the subject of her twenty-year-old self, already deemed by Bathsheve a hopeless old spinster but saved in the end by a mischievous Providence which, to spite her mother perhaps, wills otherwise. A famed itinerant preacher, one Gedalya Kreitman, serving as a fundraiser for the ultra-Orthodox Agudath Israel organisation, was looking for a bride. No, not for his potbellied self, but for his son Avraham who, to escape conscription in the tsarist army, has been sent away to Antwerp, there to receive training as a diamond-cutter.

Reb Gedalya, when in Warsaw, pays daily calls on Hindele and engages her in discussion, for she is well versed in overheard Torah and Talmud. To her mother she says: "You wish to see the back of me. Very well, I shall go into exile." A marriage is arranged, to take place in a kosher hotel in Berlin - all expenses to be defrayed by Reb Gedalya, who puts up a goodly dowry and, in a further departure from custom, bedecks his prospective daughter-in-law with costly jewels.

On the train ride into exile Hindele carries in her handbag the half-dozen notebooks which she has filled with short stories and earlier shown to her mother who has read them with raised red eyebrows and without comment. Now the mother, Bathsheve, murmurs her fear that tsarist frontier officers might sniff sedition in the Yiddish script. So Hindele does to the notebooks what she feels like doing to herself - she tears them up and flings the tattered shreds out of the window into green pastures where cows graze.

In the kosher hotel in Berlin, Hindele and Avraham meet and exchange nods. Next, they are escorted to a photographer's studio. And on the morrow they are married.

Before taking her place under the wedding canopy, Hindele lends an ear to a whisper from her father Reb Pinhas Menahem: "Do not be shy with your husband. What he and you will be doing is prescribed by the Torah, a holy act, of which your mother cannot have enough; she wears me out night after night."

I am proof that the nuptials were consummated.

One morning in the summer of 1926, the continental express carrying me and my mother pulls into the Warsaw railway terminal. There on the platform waiting for his sister Hindele is my uncle Yitzhak. I have never seen him before, but I recognise *der roiter* instantly, so unmistakable is his resemblance to Bathsheve as pictured in my mother's stories. Not so my shortsighted mother, who discovers her brother's presence only after the kisses he has vaguely darted at her fail to land on either cheek. Of me he takes no notice.

We follow my uncle into a dilapidated old train, which chugs slowly out of town. With the elusive Yitzhak my habitually over-effusive mother is at a loss for words. After half an hour or so, we alight in a pine forest on burning hot sands strewn with pine cones; the air is heady with pine sap and bird-song; the golden sun in the bluest sky I have ever seen spreads light and shade with the absoluteness peculiar to dreams. Euphoric, I exult in the fulfilment of a wish so precious as to have been kept hidden even from myself. We enter a fenced-in pinewood estate, approach a bungalow, and the waking dream takes an uncanny turn.

No longer is it Yitzhak at our side. He has flown off and been replaced by a taller and older self, still slim but not the scraggy, elusive, ethereal youth who has escorted us thus far; his gaunt face has become handsome; the ears still stick out, but they no longer look like the wings of a bat about to fly off; the massive bulging cranium has lost its mop of red hair; and, most notable of all, that indifferent faraway gaze has given way to a strange, a very strange, glitter in the whites of the eyes conveying absolute authority and absolute melancholy.

This, of course, is none other than my uncle Shiya. With a shriek of mingled joy and pain my mother throws herself upon him in an embrace so absolute as to be more than sisterly. With a struggle he disengages himself, takes a backward step, and fixes her with a glare that blends compassion with revulsion, a look which cautions his sister to understand that though pity may have moved him to invite her to a family reunion, she had best not delude herself into thinking she can thrust herself upon him for good, for already she has made a pest of herself and the sooner she goes back to where she came from, back to her unloved husband in London, the better.

My mother blinks frenziedly and bites her underlip to keep silent. For the rest of our stay she will hold herself aloof from Shiya, will look down on his wife Genya as unworthy of him, will ignore and be ignored by Yitzhak, will consort with the dacha literati and their womenfolk, and will have little to say to me. As of now, her past is a closed book and I have ceased to be her audience.

There are no dacha children my own age, so I strike up a friendship of sorts with seventeen-year-old Uri, who spends entire days over Hebrew manuals in preparation for *aliyah*, ascent to the land of Israel. The sport I revel in is uncle-watching, and it seems to have many practitioners. The dacha hums with talk of the rapport between the two Singer brothers. There is little love for the older Shiya. Again and again I, the eavesdropper, hear the same refrain: young Yitzhak will one day outstrip (the Yiddish term is *ibervaksn*, grow taller than) his older brother.

That Shiya's recently published short-story collection, *Perl* (Pearls), lives up to its title is an accepted fact, and one that goes unchallenged. But he is begrudged the stroke of good fortune that has come with it. On the strength of this first published book he has been made a correspondent for the *New York Jewish Daily Forward*, and has thereby leaped overnight from destitution to affluence. The envy this has aroused is natural, but far from natural is the gut animosity he provokes in the many, as is also the fascination he exerts on the few who are spellbound in their devotion to him.

The dacha literati take it for granted that Yitzhak belongs to the unloving majority but chooses to act like one of the devoted few. Shiya behaves like a patronising but protective father to Yitzhak, who assumes the part of a meek son and protégé. The smart alecks would have it that behind this display is a sophisticated variant of the Cain and Abel theme: I J Singer is jealous of Yitzhak's potentially superior talent, and to nip it in the bud tries to stifle him with condescending kindness. But Yitzhak, say the observers, is not fooled and, as soon as it suits him, will let his simmering resentment explode.

I listen and I wonder.

Happily, I am charged by my aunt Genya with the daily chore of fetching my two uncles to lunch. First I set out to find Yitzhak. He spends his mornings aloft in one pine tree or another, and part of the fun is locating the particular tree. What does he do up there? He reads Yiddish, Hebrew,

Polish and German prose and poetry and also studies philosophy, especially Spinoza and Kant. How do I know, since he has no *maga massa* with me, meaning in cockney idiom that he would not touch me with a bargepole? I hear it from the literati who are waiting for him to climb down and favour them with one of his impersonations. When he chooses to perform one of these, they say, there is not a clown the length and breadth of Poland who can hold a candle to my uncle Yitzhak.

When Yitzhak proves deaf to my call for lunch (I shall have to come back a second time), I run off and climb the ladder to the loft where, beneath a broken roof on which birds nest, my other uncle, Shiya, is busy writing. He sits on a stool before a bare wooden shelf which serves as his desk. Bemused, I watch his pen glide over a sheet of foolscap forming line after line of graceful script with never a pause. No, on second thought, he does pause now and then to change a word which is then smoothly traced onto an earlier sheet.

I stand behind his stooped back, and there is something in his posture which expresses what I have come to know about him. Already on the eve of my mother's departure for Berlin, Shiya was in revolt against the ancestral beliefs and customs. With the outbreak of the Bolshevik Revolution he, the messianic atheist, was off to Russia to help free the proletariat from oppression and establish heaven on earth. But the apparatchiks running the Yiddish press and publishing houses there had no use for him, who could neither fawn nor intrigue nor wink at corruption, and they flung his *Perl* novellas back at him as unfit for print. Disappointed first in Kiev, then in Moscow, he returned to Warsaw and triumphed. There is an aura of mastery about him now, but also a daunting melancholy that seems innate and inborn. Is his melancholy the cause of, or exacerbated by, the malevolence that surrounds him? I do not formulate the question - it emanates from him, hovers in the air.

One day, suddenly, Shiya turns to me and asks whether the language in which I think is Yiddish or English. I ponder the question and answer truthfully that my thoughts do not seem to be in any language at all. The whites of his eyes flash suspicion as well as melancholy: is this some kind of tomfoolery or chutzpah to get back at him perhaps for my mother's sake? Or am I just an honest imbecile!? Either way, he regrets having addressed me and will never do so again.

Perhaps, if he had not turned away so impetuously, I might have had a chance to collect my wits and explain that in his company and, indeed, throughout this summer at the dacha, I am too happy for words. Only when I am angry do I think in words and I do not now have it in me to take umbrage or even to feel sorry for my mother - I am busy reaping a harvest of impressions too rich to be ground and milled into verbal flour or kneaded and baked into the bread of common sense.

I run off to give my uncle Yitzhak his second call for lunch, knowing that when I find him he will be up a tree - in this case both literally and figuratively. (The Yiddish equivalent would be *er hengt in der luftn*, he hangs in midair.) For the time being he is a young man of high promise but humble achievement. Under a variety of pseudonyms - he has not yet become Bashevis - he dashes off merciless reviews of books and plays, has started on a Yiddish translation of Thomas Mann's *The Magic Mountain*, and tosses off cheap heartthrob romances for serialisation in the daily press. He is scandalously underpaid, but as a strict vegetarian as well as a non-smoker, a non-boozer (albeit not a teetotaller), and a philanderer besieged by mistresses costing not a zloty, his expenses are negligible.

The literati at the foot of the tree reckon that Yitzhak is under a constraint. Storytelling will be his forte, but he aspires to originality, and to make his mark as a groundbreaker he will have to draw on much the same wellspring of experience as his brother I J Singer, who has had a head start. Never mind, say the literati, he will have it in him to overcome this handicap on two scores. First, he will dig into himself for the inspiration to weave that shared life experience into a new, unique pattern. Second, he is bursting with impatience to "grow taller" than his brother and eventually overshadow him.

In the years and decades ahead, these speculations will come back to me, but meanwhile there I am at the foot of the pine tree, down which Yitzhak comes slithering, agile as a squirrel. Once on the ground, he is surrounded by the literati begging for an impersonation and offering a choice among three local celebrities - a nutty mystic, a pompous essayist, and an alcoholic poet (one whose talent compares favourably with Heine's and whose name will one day grace a Tel Aviv street; but of this, as of so much else, I have not the faintest premonition).

Yitzhak strikes a comic scarecrow pose, as if pondering whom best to mimic. Slowly the seconds - or is it minutes? - pass until we suddenly become aware that he is no longer there, that he has vanished from under our very noses like a phantom. How did it happen? Did he take advantage of an instant's inattention, or has he lulled his audience into a trance? Heads turn in all directions, but there is no Yitzhak and there will be no burlesque.

Not long after, as though to make up for it, my mother and I are treated in private to a memorable scene of real-life tragicomedy. The occasion is a visit to the theatre. Yitzhak has invited the two of us to see a Yiddish farce running in Warsaw called *Redaktor Katchke* (Editor Duck). The play, aside from its funny title (*Katchke* is the Yiddish equivalent of the French canard, meaning a whopping journalistic lie), consists of only one gag, endlessly repeated and unfailingly raising a laugh. Each time the apoplectic editor opens his mouth he lets loose a deluge of spittle, obliging the other characters to shield themselves with straw hats or parasols.

Squeezed into one seat with my mother (my uncle has obtained only two free tickets for the three of us), I find my attention straying to Yitzhak who does not, I notice, give the stage so much as a single glance. Evidently he considers this cheap fare good enough for us, while he himself gazes off into nothingness. This once I really want to be angry with him, but again I simply cannot - he is out of my reach, absent. So constant is this air of his that at table it would not be surprising to see him pour a spoonful of soup into his ear instead of his mouth. But he never does. In a pinch he is all there. From the way his temples twitch, the way he blushes and breaks out in a clammy sweat, it is plain that all manner of potent, contradictory forces are clashing within him and liable to throw him into convulsions. But somehow the warring powers arrive at a standoff so that, for all his feverish restlessness, he still keeps his poise.

After the show, he takes us to Shiya's apartment on elegant Leszno Street, where we spend the night. Early the next morning, back from a shopping errand, my mother and I enter with a borrowed front-door key and we are greeted by an astonishing sight. There in the hall, on the polished parquet floor, stands Yitzhak suffering what looks to be a crucifixion of sorts. His arms are stretched out to their full length and effectively nailed in place by, on the one side, a skinny young woman who has dug her fingernails into the wrist she is clutching and, on the other side, a more buxom one who is doing the same. Each wants him wholly to herself. They wage a desperate tug of war, which bids fair to split him clean down the middle, half a Yitzhak being better than none. His gaunt, flushed face is wreathed in the torment of a mock-martyr.

The outcome? Events will follow their set course. The buxom maiden Runya will bear Yitzhak a son who, along with his mother, will be sent packing. Many years later, the son, Yisrael, will Hebraise the surname Singer into Zamir, and become a kibbutznik and editor of the leftist daily *Al Hamishmar*. I shall meet up with him in a Tel Aviv hotel room where he has been ignored and kept waiting by his estranged father, Yitzhak. But more of that later.

On another early morning in that summer of 1926, who is it I see between the pine trees, taking gingerly steps on the hot sand, but my grandmother Bathsheve? She has arrived during the night with my grandfather, Reb Pinhas Menahem, from their distant Galician *shtetl* of Zykow Stary (whither they had fled with young Moshe from troubled Warsaw during the Great War).

There is less - but also more - to Bathsheve than the word-picture that has been imprinted in my mind. Age, I suppose, has shrivelled to nothing what little flesh was on her frame, now quite skeletal but still erect; her neck is scrawny beyond belief; the once-fiery red eyebrows are faded, the wig she wears is dark, deepening the mystery of how such a gaunt little face can accommodate such enormous, sunken eyes, such sharp cheekbones, so prominent a nose, and so upturned a chin. And, mystery of mysteries, how can so small and birdlike a head contain a brain capable of storing all those volumes of Torah, Talmud and kabbalah, not to mention that burden of agonised grievance she carries around with her against Jehovah her Maker, soured with unmotherly ruthlessness and spiced with sardonic scorn of commoners deemed lesser spirits than her exalted self?

My grandmother is accompanied by Shiya, who retreats at the approach of his sister, my mother, Hindele.

In their first encounter since parting in Berlin so many years before, mother and daughter go through the motions of a tepid embrace. Then the mother says to the daughter: "Why, Hindele, you are not at all as ugly as I thought you were!" Next my grandmother, thin lips pursed and the same greyish colour as her enormous eyes, bestows a first (and last) icy glance at myself, a lad of barmitzvah age, shockingly bareheaded and bare-legged, shamelessly bereft of ear-locks and ritual fringes.

My grandparents do not take their meals with the family, but now and then I sight my grandfather Reb Pinhas Menahem, whose appearance is everything I expected - and more so. Frail, he has the dainty tread of a ballerina in rabbinic garb: black caftan, black skullcap, ritual fringes, golden ear-locks bobbing to and fro, and a wavy golden beard glued to a sweet girlish face.

One evening, when the pinewood glows scarlet in the sunset, he musters the courage to approach me, unseen by Bathsheve. Within touching distance but at arm's length he stops and gazes, in quest, I suppose, of some small resemblance to the Singer family. I gaze back. Never before have I seen, nor shall I ever see again, such childlike lovingness in a grown man, or such a look of innocence but also wisdom as in those gentle blue eyes. Still within touching distance but without touching, he says in a tremolo: "I dearly love your mother Hindele, and you, Moshe, her dear son, I dearly love also." And with that he turns away.

In the course of this visit I come to hear much sorrowful talk of my namesake Moshe, the youngest Singer brother. It has pleased Bathsheve to report that her beloved Moshe is so pious he decided not to make the journey to the family reunion, lest he find himself rubbing shoulders with a female in a crowded train compartment. To which Shiya, through gritted teeth, responds: "Our mother has had her way and crushed his spirit." And Yitzhak adds in a tone of resignation: "Our mother congratulates herself on having saved his soul from the everlasting hellfire into which her other sons, you and I, will be cast."

My two uncles agree that Moshe is another genius. His is far and away the best scholarly brain in the family. They relate how, after celebrating his bar mitzvah, Moshe set about organising a Zionist youth movement, travelling far and wide over Galicia to enlist recruits. A born leader and orator, he preached the return to the Promised Land in synagogues after evening prayers. But then his mother got to work on him. "Our mother has snuffed out the will to live in her Moishele, she has buried him alive," says my mother, indignant but not the least surprised.

What surprises me, however, is my uncle Yitzhak's aloofness from his mother Bathsheve. He exchanges only a few offhand remarks with her and, in so doing, his eyes wear the same chill, steely glaze as her own. But he spends hours on end communing with, or rather listening to, his father Reb Pinhas Menahem. And something of his father's tenderness, wonder, awe, and delight flushes Yitzhak's own face, tempered or spiced with amusement. He seems to be feasting on the wonders and miracles of Hasidic lore.

One day my grandparents leave the same way they came - unannounced. I presume my mother has seen them off, but she does not speak of it. And soon after, it is our turn to leave as well. My uncle Yitzhak takes us to the Warsaw train station, and once again the kisses he darts at my mother's cheek miss their mark. She and I stand together in the corridor of the train. She waves goodbye through the open window, but thanks to her short-sightedness fails to see that he has vanished from the platform.

Yiddish literature has been permanently enriched by Isaac Bashevis Singer's masterly novel, *Satan in Goray*, set in seventeenth-century Poland and describing how the remnants of Jewry after the Chmielnicki pogroms fall prey to rabid superstition. The horrors are presented without that *nebbish* whine - with no pathos. There is to the tale the vividness, the intensity, of an eerily entertaining nightmare which overcomes the reader, oblivious of the author who keeps himself aloof throughout. In style and spirit, in that book as well as in the many others he would write in his lifetime - from *The Family Moskat* through *The Slave*, *The Spinoza of Market Street*, *The Manor*, and on and on - he is a storyteller like no other.

As for the elder brother I J Singer, after the period I have just spoken of his reputation in Yiddish went on to soar triumphantly - after one brief melodramatic fall. Critics vented their spleen on the war novel which followed *Perl* (and which appeared in English in my translation under the title *Blood Harvest*). Stung, he retorted with an absurd public "renunciation of Yiddish literature", a renunciation he later renounced with two splendid novels, *Yoshe Kalb* and *The Brothers Ashkenazi*. A stage version of *Yoshe Kalb*, starring Maurice Schwartz, became the biggest hit in the history of the Yiddish theatre. It also led Shiya to move to New York, from where he was later able to provide a haven for Yitzhak from the oncoming Holocaust.

My mother, who had been the first of the Singer siblings to take up the pen, earned recognition as well under her married name of Esther Kreitman. Her autobiographical novel, *Der Sheydim-tants* (The Demons' Dance), was published first in Warsaw and later came out in my English translation under the title *Deborah*. Long after her death this novel would be resuscitated, thanks to the English writer Clive Sinclair, who would "discover" her while doing research for his excellent study, *The Brothers Singer*. Since then *Deborah* has gone on to a second life in Britain and the United States, and has also appeared in French and German, with a Danish version in the offing.

In 1938, my uncle Yitzhak made his English debut in an anthology I edited, *Jewish Short Stories of Today*. The compilation was - mea culpa - a family vehicle in disguise, with contributions signed by Isaac Bashevis Singer, I J Singer, Esther Kreitman, and my own pseudonym of Martin Lea, which I adopted for a London dockland novel, *The House of Napolitano*.

Not long after the publication of this anthology (to turn back again from literary matters to more personal ones), my own biography took a turn for the better when the Yiddish author A M Fuchs, in flight from post-Anschluss Vienna, came to our London apartment to pay a courtesy call on my mother, the writer. Accompanying him on the visit was his daughter Lola, to whom I surrendered my chastity, and who not long after became my wife and the mother of our daughter Hazel, born in the middle of World War II. While Lola was in labour, I, a civilian, sat in a second-floor office on Fleet Street in bombed-out London, monitoring German and French radio broadcasts.

The year is 1945, the war is won; among the lost are six million Jewish men, women, and children. I am now working for the Reuters news agency as a roving correspondent in Europe and North Africa and am quartered, along with Lola, Hazel, and my mother, who is visiting from London, in the five-star Chatham Hotel near the Place de l'Opera in Paris. One day my uncle Yitzhak arrives for a visit. Climbing the stairs and avoiding the elevator as is his wont, he reaches our landing, only to find my mother in hysterics, a malady which has come to afflict her in place of her previous bouts of epilepsy. Ordinarily, these fits must simply run their course to the point of exhaustion, but at his command, "Don't upset the *kinder!*" she recovers her composure.

Converted to Zionism by my coverage of the Nazi war-crimes trials, I quit Reuters but stay on in Paris where Yitzhak looks me up whenever he is in town, and deplores my lapse from storytelling to journalism. "Write," he urges me, "and get yourself a mistress who lives in an attic. The thrill, the expectancy you will feel on the upstairs climb, will turn you on."

Did my uncle urge me to become a storyteller? Very well, I do now have a story to tell, and here it is. One day, I am hurrying along the Boulevard Bonne Nouvelle, meaning the Boulevard of Good Tidings (this is fact, not fiction), when I suddenly hear the sound of an odd but somehow familiar name - the name "Jambul" - or do I simply imagine having heard it? I stop short in the busy throng and catch sight of a short, stocky man leaning against a shop window, wearing a trilby hat with its brim lowered just enough to leave one eye uncovered. And yes, he is speaking Yiddish to a companion. I go up to the stranger and ask whether he did in fact just say the name "Jambul". His watery eye in its drooping sac looks me over, and he nods assent.

Jambul is a place somewhere in Siberia, one of the new towns built by slave labour in Russia's frozen north. My grandparents and my uncle Moshe were deported there from the Galician *shtetl* which became part of the Russian-occupied zone when Stalin and Hitler partitioned Poland in 1939. At the end of the war, my mother, living in London, received three postcards from her mother in Jambul informing her that Bathsheve and Moshe were there together. To the name of Pinhas Menahem, her husband, my grandmother had appended the Hebrew initials denoting "of blessed memory", but where and how he died she did not say. There was never a fourth postcard.

"Were you in Jambul?" I ask the watery-eyed stranger, who again nods in assent. "I have an uncle Moshe Singer who is living there with his mother Bathsheve. Did you happen to meet them?"

"You had an uncle Moshe Singer," the stranger half-chortles, half-snarls. "The *shmoyger* (nincompoop) didn't have the gumption to get organised, so he let himself starve and freeze to death. Did his wife hate him? Oh my, how she hated him? Children? No children. His mother? When I left, she was still around, but not for long, I guess."

I do not believe in Satan, but there he stands, incarnate, with only one watery eye showing from beneath the turned-down brim of his trilby. I do not believe in predestination, but how else am I to account for these ill tidings received that day on the misnamed Boulevard Bonne Nouvelle? I walk away, blaming my grandmother Bathsheve for the death of my uncle Moshe, my namesake, and for my own birth.

Uncle Yitzhak, when I tell him of this encounter, listens with bowed head. The muscles of his gaunt face register a tremor. His lips move for words uttered in silence.

Many years later my uncle Yitzhak comes to visit us in Tel Aviv, where we are now living and where we have an apartment on Hayarkon Street overlooking the Mediterranean. He inspects the oil paintings done in two very different styles by Lola and Hazel, lingering over and finally accepting as a gift one of Hazel's canvases depicting a bearded Jew brooding over an empty chessboard. The mood of this last visit is a tender one, but the idyll is soon to come to an abrupt, grotesque end.

Some months after this I receive an unexpected phone call. To my surprise, Yitzhak is in Tel Aviv again, staying at the Park Hotel, and he wishes me to present myself the following morning at nine o'clock sharp to start work on a joint translation of his newly completed novel. I arrive punctually but have been preceded by Yitzhak's son, Yisrael Zamir - a reminder that my uncle is also a father.

On my entry, Yitzhak motions me to a chair and begins reading aloud from the manuscript resting on his lap. As he reads, sentence by sentence, my job is to translate aloud into English without losing the Yiddish flavour. Having no notion of what the next sentence is to be, let alone what story is about to unfold, I begin to flounder, whereupon Bashevis snaps at me, "Simple, simple, keep it simple!" - even as he keeps taking down the sentences I dictate one by one. This goes on for fully two hours, at which point Yisrael Zamir, cooling his heels and totally ignored all this time, approaches, looms over his seated father, and snarls: "Now I see how you came to write *The Slave!*"

The next day uncle Yitzhak comes to my apartment unannounced. He sits down at the foot of a couch and, head lowered, hands compressed between his knees, begins brooding. After a longish interval he pronounces judgment: "Your mother was a madwoman." I have a delayed reaction, but a violent one. The following day my uncle is waiting for me outside the Park Hotel where he is being interviewed in Hebrew by a woman journalist and I walk past him without a greeting. The grimace of pained astonishment distorting his face reminds me of my mother on her deathbed, swinging around aghast to draw her very last breath.

Thinking back on it now, I am a fool for having broken with my uncle Yitzhak. In spite of everything he did dedicate a novel to his sister, though the dedication managed to get her name slightly wrong (Minda Esther, instead of Hinde Esther), a misprint which he attributed to her *sheydim* - her demons. After all this was over, Yitzhak's wife and ideal life-companion Alma, who knew enough to treat him as a storyteller first and last, and only incidentally (and discreetly) as a husband, gently remonstrated with me. She wrote me a letter explaining that when Yitzhak said wild things he was merely rehearsing possible themes for a story.

The warring personalities inhabiting my uncle Yitzhak's slight frame enriched the compositions, the harmonic flights, of the storyteller Isaac Bashevis Singer. Those literati who foretold, when Yitzhak was still up a tree, that he would "dig into himself" to tap to the full his latent storytelling gifts overlooked the streak of shyness in his makeup which inhibited self-portrayal. More's the pity, for his was a truly fascinating character.

Those same literati were as wrong as wrong could be in their forecast of an oncoming storm, a cloudburst of Yitzhak's seething resentment, even outright hatred, against his elder brother Shiya. In the event, Yitzhak maintained a compulsive, lifelong posture of worshipfulness toward Shiya, publicly, demonstratively, in and out of season, referring to him as "my master". Here was an enigma, behaviour so utterly unlike his customary self or selves - whatever the complexity of his character, submissiveness was no part of it - as to suggest a case of hypnosis. Far-fetched? Perhaps, though ultimately Yitzhak did see fit to come out with a confession that not until the lamented death of his senior brother did he feel altogether free, "free as a bird", to spread his literary wings.

That Yitzhak Bashevis himself exerted hypnotic powers, I can attest, and so surely can many others who found his presence spellbinding. That he himself should have been charmed by Shiya, the melancholy Shiya, and have trod so warily in order never, never to hurt him, was just one of those anomalies that go to make up the turning, twisted web of life, and also the novels and short stories, of Isaac Bashevis Singer.

My uncle Yitzhak was not a believer in the betterment of the human species. He voiced his irreproachable philosophy, uttered his ultimate *mot juste*, over that stinking hard-boiled egg in a sweet-smelling pinewood forest in Poland: "Such, yes, such is life."

*Commentary, December* 1992

# Glossary

**bime**     raised platform in the synagogue on which the reading desk stands

**Brivele der Mamen, Rozhinkes mit Mandlen** "A Letter to My Mama" and "Raisins and Almonds" - two popular Yiddish songs

**challah**     braided egg-bread, traditionally eaten on the Sabbath and at festivals

**cheder**     traditionally, a full-time elementary religious school for Jewish children. These days *cheder* usually refers to religious education classes outside school hours

**cholent**     traditional Sabbath dish; slow-cooked meat and bean stew

**chuppah (Yid. khupe)** wedding canopy or wedding ceremony

**Eyn Yankev** title of a popular book of biblical commentary from the sixteenth century. A simplified version of the *Gemara*, part of the Talmud

**Gaon**     outstanding rabbinical scholar

**golem**     legendary creature made out of clay and brought to life by magical means to help Jews avert disaster in times of trouble; behaving like an automaton

**goy (pl. goyim)** non-Jew(s), Gentile(s); can be used pejoratively

**grobe kishke** baked dish, made of meat, flour and spices, stuffed into a casing made of intestines

**Haggodah**  collection of historical and biblical texts, psalms and songs, recited at the Seder

**Hasid (pl. Hasidim)** member of a Jewish religious movement founded in the eighteenth century in Eastern Europe, organised into groupings devoted to particular rabbis, stressing pious devotion and ecstasy more than learning

**havdolah**  ceremony marking the end of the Sabbath and the beginning of a new week

**heymish**  homely, warm, cosy, traditional setting

**kharoset**  brown, sweet paste (made from apples, nuts, spices and wine) eaten at Passover

**Kol Nidre**  first service of Yom Kippur, the Day of Atonement, when the penitent seeks forgiveness for unfulfilled vows

**mamzer**  bastard

**Ma nishtane ha' layla ha'ze** "Why is this night different from all other nights?" The first of four questions asked by the youngest person present at a Seder ceremony

**mazl tov**  congratulations; literally, good luck

**menorah**  seven-branched candelabrum

**minyan**  quorum of ten (traditionally) males over thirteen years of age required for communal worship and certain ceremonies. Literally: number

**Mishna**  collection of laws and rabbinical discussions; part of the Talmud

**misnaged**  opponent of Hasidism

**Reb**  used as a title of respect for a man; could be applied to a small-town rabbi who does not have rabbinic qualifications; comparable to "Mr" in English, but usually prefixed to a first name

**Rebbe**  Hasidic spiritual leader, my master

**rebbetsin**     rabbi's wife

**Rosh Hashonah** Jewish New Year

**Seder**     ceremonial meal for the celebration of Passover, during which the story of the Exodus from Egypt is told

**shammes**     caretaker of a synagogue; rabbi's personal assistant

**Shema**     prayer which starts with the words *Shema Yisrael*, "Hear O Israel", recited as part of the morning and evening prayers as well as before bedtime

**shidduch**     arranged marriage; match (with the intention of marriage)

**shikse**     non-Jewish woman; can be used pejoratively

**shlemiel**     awkward, simple person

**shtetl**     small Eastern European town or village with a Jewish population

**tallis**     striped, tasselled, white shawl worn by Jews during certain prayers

**tsimes**     vegetable/fruit stew

**yarmulke**     head covering worn by orthodox male Jews at all times, and by others during prayer

**yeshiva**     rabbinical seminary; a school devoted to religious study

**yid**     Jew, can be used pejoratively

**yidene**     Jewish woman

**yikhes**     Jewish nobility, of good family, good family background

**Sylvia Paskin** lectures on film and literature and teaches creative writing. She has both edited and co-edited several books on film, fiction and poetry: *Angels of Fire*, *Dancing the Tightrope*, *Dybbuk of Delight*, *The Slow Mirror* and *When Joseph Met Molly*. She works as literary editor for David Paul Publishing.

**Dorothee van Tendeloo** is a freelance translator and literary critic specialising in twentieth century Yiddish, Hebrew and European literature. Her published essays in English include articles on S Y Agnon and Esther Kreitman in *Jewish Writers of the Twentieth Century*. She has translated into Dutch for Vassallucci publishers *Yiddish: A Nation of Words* by Miriam Weinstein and, also for Vassallucci she has translated stories from Yiddish for *Papieren Schatten* (Paper Treasures), an anthology of Yiddish literature written by women. She lives in London.